Agatha C

Love From A Stranger

Frank Vosper

based on a story by
Agatha Christie

A SAMUEL FRENCH ACTING EDITION

SAMUEL
FRENCH
FOUNDED 1830

SAMUELFRENCH.COM
SAMUELFRENCH-LONDON.CO.UK

FOR PRODUCTION ENQUIRIES

UNITED STATES AND CANADA

Info@SamuelFrench.com

1-866-598-8449

UNITED KINGDOM AND EUROPE

Theatre@SamuelFrench-London.co.uk

020-7255-4302

Each title is subject to availability from Samuel French, depending upon country of performance. Please be aware that *LOVE FROM A STRANGER* may not be licensed by Samuel French in your territory. Professional and amateur producers should contact the nearest Samuel French office or licensing partner to verify availability.

MUSIC USE NOTE

Licensees are solely responsible for obtaining formal written permission from copyright owners to use copyrighted music in the performance of this play and are strongly cautioned to do so. If no such permission is obtained by the licensee, then the licensee must use only original music that the licensee owns and controls. Licensees are solely responsible and liable for all music clearances and shall indemnify the copyright owners of the play(s) and their licensing agent, Samuel French, against any costs, expenses, losses and liabilities arising from the use of music by licensees. Please contact the appropriate music licensing authority in your territory for the rights to any incidental music.

IMPORTANT BILLING AND CREDIT REQUIREMENTS

If you have obtained performance rights to this title, please refer to your licensing agreement for important billing and credit requirements.

LOVE FROM A STRANGER was first produced at the New Theatre, St. Martin's Lane, London, W.C.2, by Murray Macdonald on March 31st, 1936. The cast was as follows:

LOUISE GARRARD................................ Muriel Aked

MAVIS WILSON.................................. Norah Howard

CECILY HARRINGTON .... Marie Ney

BRUCE LOVELL...................................Frank Vosper

NIGEL LAWRENCE............................... Geoffrey King

HODGSON .... Charles Hodges

ETHEL.. Esma Cannon

DR. GRIBBLE ....S. Major Jones

CHARACTERS

LOUISE GARRARD
MAVIS WILSON
CECILY HARRINGTON
BRUCE LOVELL
NIGEL LAWRENCE
HODGSON
ETHEL
DR. GRIBBLE

SETTING

ACT ONE
Scene I: Cecily and Mavis's flat in Bayswater. Early in March.
Scene II: The same. Two hours later.

ACT TWO
Scene I: The cottage. Six weeks later.
Scene II: The same. September.

ACT THREE
Scene I: The same. A fortnight later.
Scene II: The same. Forty minutes later.

ACT ONE

Scene I

(Scene – The sitting-room of a "flat," which is actually the top floor of a house in Bayswater.)

(At the moment it is being prepared for being "let furnished," certain more personal treasures are being packed away in a small trunk which is in the middle of the room.)

(LOUISE GARRARD (AUNTIE LOO-LOO) is bending over the trunk, presenting a fair and square view of her lower dorsal curves to the audience as she does so. She is a professional "fusser." She holds her inelegant pose for quite a long time, then straightens herself.)

AUNTIE LOO-LOO. *(to the trunk)* You're finished; now you can go out on the landing.

(She opens the door up right centre, takes the trunk out on to the landing and returns. She shuts the door and crosses to the mantelpiece, collecting a duster from the centre table as she does so.)

Now, then, what's the next thing to be done? *(She picks up two candlesticks from the mantelpiece and calls to someone in the next room.)* You surely aren't going to leave these lovely candlesticks out, Mavis? *(She takes the candlesticks to the centre table and starts to dust them.)*

MAVIS. *(off)* What?

AUNTIE LOO-LOO. *The candlesticks!* You'll want them packed away, won't you?

MAVIS. *(off)* Do you think so?

AUNTIE LOO-LOO. *(wrapping one candlestick up in newspaper which is on the table)* Well, you know what strange servants are – if the people who take the flat keep a servant – maids are so clumsy and heavy-handed these days. *(dusting the second candlestick)* I can remember them ever since I was quite a tiny tot. My mother – Cecily's grandmother, you know – used to say they were absolutely unique. *(She starts to wrap the second candlestick in newspaper.)* The Garrards always had *such* good taste. I remember – *(She drops the second candlestick, which breaks.)* Oh, dear me!

MAVIS. *(off)* What was that?

AUNTIE LOO-LOO. Nothing, dear; nothing. *(She picks up the candlestick which is broken in two and snatches up a piece of newspaper.)* Somehow one of the candlesticks slipped through my fingers slightly. *(She quickly wraps up the pieces.)*

MAVIS. *(off)* Is it damaged?

AUNTIE LOO-LOO. *(looking at the parcel)* Er – no – er – not noticeably.

*(The telephone rings on the small table left. **AUNTIE LOO-LOO** crosses to answer it.)*

(very loudly) Hullo? Hullo?... Yes – no – er – that is, I don't know. *(shouting into the other room)* Mavis, what is this number? I never can remember.

MAVIS. *(off)* Two three eight three.

AUNTIE LOO-LOO. *(into the 'phone)* Oh, yes, yes, this is two three eight three... yes, that's right... flat to let – well, that is to say it's more of a maisonnette; the bathroom and the – er – is a floor lower... *(indignantly)* No, certainly not; of *course* it's not the maid speaking – the maid's away, having her wisdom teeth out. I am Miss Harrington's aunt.

*(**MAVIS**, a pleasant, calm-faced woman of about thirty, with a firm manner, enters from the bedroom up left centre with a small drawer and sheets, etc. She puts these on the table centre and exits into the bedroom again.*

She returns with more linen, closing the door after her, and puts this other linen on the table. She crosses down to the bureau right to fetch a notebook and pencil, then returns to the centre table and starts checking the linen. Meanwhile **AUNTIE LOO-LOO** *has been carrying on her conversation at the telephone.)*

I'm helping my niece and her friend get the place ready for tenants... Oh, yes, it's furnished, beautifully furnished – you want it furnished?... Well, then, that's splendid, isn't it?... Oh, you don't want it furnished... but I don't understand, this is a *furnished flat (in a piercing whisper to* **MAVIS***)* Someone inquiring about the flat. *(Into the 'phone.)* But I really can't understand – you don't mean to tell me that the house-agents... no, no; this is to be let furnished!...

*(***MAVIS*** *moves round right of the table and below the sofa to left of* **AUNTIE LOO-LOO.***)*

How dare you! I'm not shouting!... *(handing the telephone to* **MAVIS***)* Here, Mavis, please deal with this; they're being so tiresome – some muddle-headed woman! *(stooping to get under the telephone flex)* Silly fool!

MAVIS. *(calmly, into the 'phone)* Hullo – yes... yes... No, I'm afraid not... quite so... good-bye. *(She hangs up the receiver.)* Some mistake on the part of the agent.

AUNTIE LOO-LOO. *(crossing and putting away a wrapped candlestick in the cupboard up right)* Oh, I see – well, there was no necessity for the woman to be so offensive... are you quite sure those house-agents are really good?

MAVIS. *(kneeling on the sofa and checking the linen over the back of it)* They seemed as good as any house-agent can be, Miss Garrard.

AUNTIE LOO-LOO. *(returning from the cupboard to the centre table)* Well, I dare say you know best, and, of course, it's not for me to interfere. I'm merely Cecily's aunt and her only relation, but personally I always think that Harrods are the best people – *(She notices the piece of newspaper in the small drawer brought in by* **MAVIS.***)* Really,

Mavis, surely you could find something better than newspaper to line your drawer with!

MAVIS. *(standing in the angle formed by the table and sofa and looking in the drawer)* It's supposed to keep off the moth.

AUNTIE LOO-LOO. But it looks so common! A photo of that dreadful murderer, too. *(She hands the piece of newspaper to* **MAVIS,** *then takes the second candlestick to the cupboard up right.)*

MAVIS. *(faintly amused)* Really! Tall, dark and handsome. *(She puts the newspaper back into the drawer on the table.)*

AUNTIE LOO-LOO. *(returning to the table and picking up the duster)* By the bye, Cecily's being a long time over her shopping. I do hope nothing's happened to her.

MAVIS. Oh, no – she had a lot of things to get.

AUNTIE LOO-LOO. *(crossing to the fireplace with the duster – pessimistically)* The traffic is so dreadful nowadays – those red and green lights, you never know when they're going to change – *(She finds a shilling on the mantelpiece.)* What's this money doing here?

MAVIS. *(moving round to back of centre table)* Shilling for the gas.

AUNTIE LOO-LOO. Do you really think you ought to leave out those lovely vases?

MAVIS. *(taking sheets to the cupboard up right)* We can't let the place if it looks like a prison, can we? *(She puts the sheets on the chair by the cupboard.)*

AUNTIE LOO-LOO. No… no, of course not, but people are so untrustworthy nowadays.

MAVIS. There are always references. *(She takes the candlesticks from the cupboard and puts them on the window-seat.)*

AUNTIE LOO-LOO. Ah! But they can be forged. I read in the paper only the other day about a place in Soho where they even make false passports. Then, of course, Soho – all those Italians.

MAVIS. *(coming down to back of sofa)* Well, we're not quite fools.

AUNTIE LOO-LOO. *(collecting cushions from the armchair down left and piling them up on the sofa)* Oh! Mavis dear, I do hope you're not letting yourself get a little embittered?

MAVIS. Embittered?

AUNTIE LOO-LOO. Of course, I know it's very difficult for you, Cecily getting married after you've been together all this time – we're none of us as young as we were.

MAVIS. *(who is checking table mats on the back of the sofa and entering them in the notebook on the centre table)* Don't I know it! However, I've still got my teeth.

AUNTIE LOO-LOO. I think you're very wise, going away immediately after her wedding. The flat would be so depressing without Cecily to brighten it up.

MAVIS. Yes, a three-months' holiday all over Europe will be too wonderful, when I've never had more than a fortnight on the South Coast all my life – Oh, what a blessing it's been!

AUNTIE LOO-LOO. I wonder!

MAVIS. What do you mean?

AUNTIE LOO-LOO. Well, Mavis… to tell you the truth, I'm worried. About Cecily. *(She sits at right end of the sofa.)* It seems to me that winning this twenty-thousand pounds has upset her –

MAVIS. Ten thousand; she's only won half of it.

AUNTIE LOO-LOO. Well, ten thousand, then. Don't you think it's upset her?

MAVIS. Heavens, no! Why, she's been absolutely radiant about it. She was only saying –

AUNTIE LOO-LOO. No, you don't understand. I mean as regards Nigel.

(MAVIS knows what AUNTIE LOO-LOO is driving at, and is in agreement with her, though she isn't going to admit it.)

She doesn't seem in the least like a "bride-to-be."

MAVIS. What do you expect her to do? Arrange flowers all day, humming the Jewel song from "Faust" –

AUNTIE LOO-LOO. *(oversweetly)* You know, Mavis dear, sometimes I find you a little difficult to talk to.

MAVIS. *(taking a pile of linen to the cupboard)* I'm sorry.

AUNTIE LOO-LOO. I was merely suggesting that winning that Sweep together seemed to have altered Cecily's attitude to her marriage.

*(**MAVIS** comes down from the cupboard in front of the centre table and sits on the right arm of the sofa, beside* **AUNTIE LOO-LOO.***)*

I mean not to meet Nigel at the station!

MAVIS. But Nigel particularly asked her not to.

(The gas fire goes out.)

AUNTIE LOO-LOO. Of course, I know a railway station isn't a very romantic place – so many people about and all those nasty smells. I remember when I was a young girl going to meet a very dear friend of mine at London Bridge – no, Liverpool Street it was, all those bridges, because I remember they sent me over the wrong bridge and I found myself in Broad Street; and when I got back the train was in and my friend had gone – still, the intention was there. But to a girl in love – why, even Clapham Junction – Oh, dear! Now the gas has gone out. Oh, you've got some shillings, haven't you?

(She rises and goes to the fireplace. The telephone rings.)

It's your turn to be insulted, I think.

*(**MAVIS** goes to the telephone and answers it. Meanwhile* **AUNTIE LOO-LOO** *takes the shilling from the mantelpiece and puts it in the slot. After a lot of muddling with the taps she strikes a match and holds it to the fire. There is a large "POP"!* **AUNTIE LOO-LOO** *jumps at the "pop" then strikes a second match. The fire lights up and she rises.)*

(N.B. All this can be worked by a large paper bag being popped behind the fireplace. **AUNTIE LOO-LOO**'s *match can be seen if a small mirror is placed against the fender*

to reflect through the small gap beside the gas fire. The Property Man must keep his eye on the bag or he will miss it two times out of three.)

MAVIS. *(who has been speaking into the telephone during* **AUNTIE LOO-LOO***'s business with the gas fire)* Hullo?... Yes, two three eight three... What agents?... Oh, yes... yes, four rooms... furnished for three months... yes, four guineas... certainly, you can see it whenever you like...

AUNTIE LOO-LOO. *(urgently)* Not this morning, with Nigel arriving.

MAVIS. *(into the 'phone)* Let me see, perhaps this aft – Oh, no. Hullo! No! Hi! Listen – hullo, hullo! – Oh, damn! *(She puts down the receiver.)*

AUNTIE LOO-LOO. *(gloating) Now* what's happened?

MAVIS. A man coming to see the flat. I tried to stop him, but he'd rung off; he just said: "Right, I'll come round at once."

AUNTIE LOO-LOO. He must be an impulsive sort of person.

MAVIS. He had a slight American accent. *(She crosses right to the cupboard.)*

AUNTIE LOO-LOO. Ah, that would account for it. Did he tell you his name?

MAVIS. No.

AUNTIE LOO-LOO. How very odd!... But then, of course, Americans...

MAVIS. Oh, well, I don't suppose it'll matter. Nigel's train isn't due in for another hour and it'll probably be late. I read something about fog in the Channel.

AUNTIE LOO-LOO. *(pouncing)* Fog! A cousin of mine was once in collision in a fog – just off Ramsgate it was – and I remember he said –

(The front door slams.)

MAVIS. There's Cecily.

AUNTIE LOO-LOO. She'll be worn out with her shopping, when she ought to be looking her best to welcome Nigel.

(**CECILY HARRINGTON** *enters up right centre. She is about thirty. She is very pleasant-looking without possessing striking looks – she is prettier now than she has ever been in her life before, because she can afford at last to spend money on her appearance. She has a load of parcels which she deposits on the table centre*)

Oh, you poor child!

CECILY. *(looking around bewildered)* Why, what's the matter?

(**MAVIS** *puts the linen finally into the cupboard.*)

AUNTIE LOO-LOO. You must be worn out. Tramping around all those shops.

CECILY. Oh, that! *(She takes off her hat.)* It was only one shop and I didn't tramp, I was conducted around, and by such a Dine young man. Isn't it amazing how really charming a good salesman can be?

AUNTIE LOO-LOO. You must have been lucky – I rarely meet one.

CECILY. Oh, Mavis, you've put all those things away. You should have let me do my share. *(She puts her coat and hat on the chair by the cupboard up right)*

MAVIS. *(laughing)* It doesn't matter. *(She shuts the cupboard, her work finished.)*

(**CECILY** *crosses to below the sofa and glances at her watch, checking it » by the clock on the mantelpiece.*)

CECILY. Is that clock right?

MAVIS. I think it's a little slow.

AUNTIE LOO-LOO. *(heavily playful)* Far too slow for little Cecily, I should imagine, eh?

CECILY. *(at the mantelpiece)* Why? *(Embarrassed as she understands.)* Oh, I see…

AUNTIE LOO-LOO. *(crossing to the bureau chair for her coat, bag and gloves)* And now I'm going to be a tactful old Auntie Loo-Loo and go out for a couple of hours. *(She begins to put on her coat. She has been wearing her hat all the time.)*

CECILY. Oh, but really, you needn't...

AUNTIE LOO-LOO. Rubbish! you'll want to be alone when Nigel arrives. *(Putting on her gloves, babbling all the time.)* Besides, I've got plenty to do. I shall go to Harrods and put this flat on their books. I don't altogether trust that agent. Then I shall lunch in their restaurant – a little sole – no, perhaps sweetbreads, and then a meringue – and be back about half-past two. You'll have both of you calmed down a bit by then, I expect.

CECILY. Calmed down?

AUNTIE LOO-LOO. The first raptures of reunion! Oh, I know all about it... *(With a grandiloquent gesture towards the door with her handbag, which gives her her next thought.)* There'll he be, standing in the doorway... Oh dear, I hope I haven't left myself short of change. *(She fiddles in her handbag.)*

CECILY. I've got some, Auntie Loo-Loo. *(She takes a one pound note out of her bag and offers it to* AUNTIE LOO-LOO *over the back of the sofa.)*

AUNTIE LOO-LOO. *(coming to back of sofa to collect it)* Oh, it's all right, dear – I shan't want all that... Well, perhaps a glass of sherry.

(She exits up right centre, after violent and muddled signals to MAVIS *from the doorway.)*

(There is a pause. The outer door slams. MAVIS *bursts into peals of laughter, in which* CECILY *joins.* MAVIS *gradually recovers.* CECILY *puts the cushions back from the sofa to the armchair left)*

MAVIS. *(coming to the table centre)* Auntie Loo-Loo is disappointed in you. *(She takes a cigarette from the box on the table and lights it.)* You're not reacting according to schedule – she wants flushed cheeks, dancing eyes and a correctly palpitating heart.

(There is a pause. CECILY *becomes serious.)*

CECILY. So do I.

MAVIS. Oh, do you?

CECILY. Oh, don't pretend to be surprised. You've had a pretty shrewd idea what my feelings have been for some time.

MAVIS. *(coming round in front of the sofa)* What is it?

CECILY. I'm – terribly worried.

MAVIS. Over Nigel?

CECILY. Yes.

MAVIS. *(sitting at right end of the sofa)* Really, Cecily, you've left it a bit late in the day to start changing –

CECILY. I can't help it. One must be honest with oneself, but it all seems so dull.

MAVIS. Dull?

CECILY. *(sitting on the left arm of the sofa)* Yes, dull... Nigel and I are fond of each other, of course.

MAVIS. Fond? My God! – What a word to get married on!

CECILY. We've known each other for years. It's such a very tepid romance.

MAVIS. Romance? What do you want? – Fun in a gondola?

CECILY. I want excitement. Life's been so deadly monotonous up to now.

MAVIS. It must have been pretty monotonous for Nigel.

CECILY. Yes, I know; but he's breaking away from it all now, coming back to England to something entirely fresh – that's just the point. The office has been my Sudan; and yours, too.

MAVIS. Yes, I know what you mean – but still –

CECILY. Day after day, year after year. Getting up in the morning, having to be at the office in time. Always the neat efficient secretary. "Yes, Sir Henry"... "No, Sir Henry"... "Certainly, Sir Henry." Going out to lunch, then rushing back. The journey home in the 'bus. I want to live – to live, before I'm grey and old and dead, and –

MAVIS. Can I get you a glass of water, dear, after all that?

CECILY. *(dropping from the arm to beside* MAVIS *on the sofa)* Oh, I know it sounds a bit silly, but subconsciously I've always craved for adventure, and then, when we won all this money, I saw that at last I'd got the chance of it. Do you know the first thing I did?

MAVIS. No, tell me.

CECILY. I meant to tell you before. I wrote to Nigel, asking him if he'd postpone our wedding.

MAVIS. Cecily, you didn't!

CECILY. After all, it was only a postponement.

MAVIS. What reason did you give him?

CECILY. I said I wanted just a little time to enjoy my freedom in my own way.

MAVIS. What did Nigel say?

CECILY. He was furious.

MAVIS. I'm not surprised.

CECILY. You know how he hates his plans being upset. To use his own words, he had it all cut and dried. We're to have one week after his arrival, for him to get clothes and arrange details, and then a special licence, a short honeymoon – in England, because he's seen nothing of it for so long – and then – Golders Green.

(There is a pause.)

MAVIS. *(rising and putting her cigarette out at centre table)* Yes, I know all that, but, after all, why not? It's what you've always planned yourself; I've heard you say a hundred –

CECILY. Yes, I know; but now I feel I want something more broadening than warming Nigel's slippers in front of the fire – just for a little while, Mavis, that's all.

MAVIS. *(sitting on the right arm of the sofa)* But, Cecily, you do love Nigel?

CECILY. That's just it. Do I? Have I ever loved Nigel? Or did I simply think he would do? That he was a means of escape from the office? It's an ugly thought – but it might be true.

MAVIS. No, you're doing yourself an injustice. You're not really serious.

CECILY. *(suddenly grave again)* I do wish I wasn't. *(She rises, crosses to the bureau, and takes a note out of the downstage small drawer, then stands in front of the bureau chair.)* Last night I wrote this to Nigel.

MAVIS. Oh, Cecily, *not* – ?

CECILY. Yes, breaking off our engagement.

MAVIS. *(rising)* But you can't, after all these years.

CECILY. Well, you know that's not all my fault. I offered to go out three years ago – I wouldn't have minded being poor. But Nigel thought it was wiser to wait. It wouldn't be fair to him to marry him as I feel at present – would it?

MAVIS. Perhaps not. But what are you proposing to do?

CECILY. Last night I was proposing to clear out of here this morning and leave this note for him when he arrives.

MAVIS. But you've changed your mind this morning?

CECILY. Yes. I've decided now to make one last appeal to Nigel to postpone the wedding. *(She puts the note back into the drawer.)*

MAVIS. What will you do in the meantime?

CECILY. Exactly what you're going to do. Travel, meet people –

MAVIS. What will you do if Nigel refuses?

CECILY. *(quietly)* I shall break with him... definitely.

(There is a long pause.)

MAVIS. *(rising)* Well, I think you're a fool!

CECILY. Please, Mavis! I'd hoped you'd back me up. We nearly always agree over most things.

MAVIS. *(taking a step towards* CECILY*)* Not over this. The wretched money has gone to your head.

CECILY. But you don't understand, it isn't only that –

MAVIS. In Nigel you've got the makings of a damn fine husband – you can't afford to turn a man like that down.

CECILY. I don't care if I never get –

MAVIS. Yes, and you needn't tell me that you're quite content to remain a spinster. I know you better. You're just being schoolgirlish.

CECILY. *(angrily, sitting in the bureau chair)* Oh, shut up!

MAVIS. You're over-excited, my girl, that's what's the matter with you. You're throwing away your chances of something sane and happy for some entirely fictitious idea of "seeing life." What on earth does that mean exactly?

CECILY. *(at a loss)* Well... well, for instance...

MAVIS. Paris, I suppose; sitting in an underground night-club, drinking *crème-de-menthe frappé,* with a lot of grey-faced degenerates.

CECILY. Don't be ridiculous!

MAVIS. *(moving up towards the bedroom door left centre)* Monte Carlo, then, with rude old gentlemen in panama hats pinching your behind in the Casino.

CECILY. Mavis!

(MAVIS has bounced into her room.)

MAVIS. *(off)* The wide open spaces; perhaps, the rolling sea; yo ho ho! and a bottle of rum! Paris in the spring – de-de-de-de-dee-dee-de-de-de-de-de-de-de – for God's sake! *(She emerges with a hat and coat, which she puts on.)* You'll end up on the boat-deck being mauled by a pimply young wireless-operator who bites his nails. *(She gets her bag and gloves from the window-seat.)*

CECILY. You're impossible – you're as bad as Auntie Loo-Loo.

MAVIS. Well, anyway, I'm going to follow her example by being "Oh, so tactful" and clearing out of the way for a bit. Nigel's bound to be here soon now, if the fog hasn't held him up.

(CECILY doesn't answer. MAVIS relents.)

Cheer up, ducky. It'll all come out in the wash.

CECILY. *(dully)* Will it? *(She looks at her.)*

MAVIS. *(smiling)* You'll see.

(She goes out up right centre)

*(Left alone, **CECILY** rises and helps herself to a cigarette from the box on the table, a box that is actually a handsomely bound volume with the inside converted to contain cigarettes. She stands lost in concentrated thought. At length she appears to make up her mind – she puts on her hat and coat with determination, crosses to the bureau, takes out the letter, places it on the mantelpiece, then goes to the door. She stands holding the handle in afresh agony of indecision. She comes back into the room, pulls off her hat and coat slowly, goes to the mantelpiece looking at the letter.)*

*(As she does so, **BRUCE LOVELL** appears quietly in the doorway. He is between thirty and thirty-five, about six feet in height, powerfully built. His appearance radiates health, and, he has very fine teeth. His hair is a strong crisp golden. His manner is a strange mixture of shyness and utter unselfconsciousness. He speaks with a slight American accent which is sufficiently soft to be attractive. He watches **CECILY** for a few moments while she removes her hat as she stands looking at the note on the mantelpiece, then he speaks.)*

BRUCE. Well, I came as quick as ever I could.

*(**CECILY** swings round startled.)*

CECILY. Ni – ! *(She realizes her mistake.)* Oh, I – I thought you were somebody else.

BRUCE. Sorry to disappoint you. *(He places his hat and mackintosh on the chair by the cupboard up right)*

CECILY. *(flummoxed)* Oh – er – not at – er – what do you – ? – er – How did you – ?

BRUCE. The door was left open, so I just walked in. I hope you don't mind?

(She stares at him, still rather nonplussed. He remains at the door.)

CECILY. Er – what – what do you want?

BRUCE. *(smiling)* You must have rather a short memory, spoke to you just now on the 'phone.

CECILY. Spoke to – ? Oh, but I'm afraid there's some mistake. I've been out all the morning. I've only just come in, and I haven't spoken to anybody on the 'phone.

BRUCE. Not about this flat of yours, that you want to rent?

CECILY. About the flat? – Oh, of course, I see, yes... I expect you spoke to my friend – she's just gone out – she must have forgotten to tell me. *(She puts her hat and coat on the armchair left.)*

BRUCE. Yes, that must be it. I thought your voice sounded rather different to the one I spoke with.

CECILY. Mavis and I are supposed to speak very much alike.

BRUCE. I prefer your voice.

(His manner is so direct that it is impossible to resent anything he says, but she is a little taken aback. There is a slight pause.)

CECILY. *(recovering herself – rather nervously)* Oh, but what am I thinking of? Won't you come in?

BRUCE. Thanks.

CECILY. *(hastily tidying the sofa)* Won't you sit down?

BRUCE. Thank you. *(He sits in the bureau chair, which has been left slightly facing into the centre of the room.)*

CECILY. I'm afraid it's a little untidy. We've been packing; you know how it is when –

BRUCE. You were expecting somebody else?

CECILY. Er – yes – er – my fiancé; he's returning from the Sudan today.

BRUCE. Oh? That's swell for you, isn't it?

CECILY. *(without enthusiasm)* Yes... well, now I'd better show you round. This – er – well, this is the sitting-room – rather an obvious remark – but there it is.

BRUCE. That's a grand table – is it real?

CECILY. Yes, we've got one or two rather nice pieces; my mother left them to me.

BRUCE. Charming atmosphere! I'm very sensitive to atmosphere, aren't you?

CECILY. I don't know.

BRUCE. I'm sure you are. I'm pretty good at summing people up quickly. I've had to be, with the sort of life I've led.

CECILY. *(intrigued)* Really – and have you summed me up already?

BRUCE. Oh, no, only slightly; you're not as easy as all that.

(He smiles at her and there is a little pause. She becomes slightly embarrassed again, and crosses to the door down left)

CECILY. *(opening it)* This is the dining-room.

(BRUCE rises, crosses and exits down left.)

BRUCE. *(off)* Very cosy. I like that picture over the mantelpiece. *(He returns.)*

CECILY. It belonged to my mother too. I think it's a picture of some place in Greece.

BRUCE. *(above the door)* It's the Gulf of Corinth. I know the exact spot.

CECILY. *(below the door)* Do you really?

BRUCE. *(looking off again at the picture)* I remember waking up very early and going up on deck in the dawn. You never saw anything so lovely – the mountains, snow-capped, then pale violet and deep mauve, reflected in the sea... and the sea cold and still like jade.

CECILY. How heavenly! *(She sighs.)* I've never travelled. *(She shuts the door.)*

BRUCE. *(strolling to centre and turning)* But you'd like to?

CECILY. It's my great ambition.

BRUCE. Everybody ought to travel, it keeps alive the spirit of adventure and that's all to the good, it seems to me. It's up to us to see all we can of the world – to appreciate it, instead of pushing it away in a lumber-room like a dud wedding present.

CECILY. *(taking a step or two towards him)* Oh, I do so agree – you know, it's funny, I shouldn't have thought you were at all – er…

BRUCE. At all what?

CECILY. Well, capable of such – er – how shall I put it? – er – self-expression.

BRUCE. I look too much of a roughneck – is that it!

CECILY. *(laughing)* No, really I meant that men of your type usually grunt and puff harder at their pipes when you draw their attention to something lovely – but you seem to have a real appreciation of beauty.

BRUCE. *(gazing at her)* I certainly have.

(CECILY, embarrassed, crosses quickly to the bedroom door.)

CECILY. You'll want to see the bedrooms, there are two of them – this way. They lead out of each other.

(He follows her out of the room, and you hear them talking offstage.)

(off) This is Miss Wilson's room. My room is through there, and I'm afraid it is rather untidy.

BRUCE. *(off)* Never mind.

CECILY. *(off)* One gets quite a nice view out of that window.

BRUCE. *(off)* Grand! Is that the park over there?

CECILY. *(off)* Yes, it's really quite charming, particularly in the spring.

BRUCE. *(off)* I'm sure it is – this is the room I shall use.

CECILY. Are you going to keep a servant? Because if you are –

(They both re-enter the room.)

I can put you on to quite a good daily woman. *(She takes the pencil and notebook which MAVIS has left on the table and crosses to the bureau.)*

BRUCE. Well, I don't know. I've been looking after myself for the last eighteen months, and I've got kind of used to it.

CECILY. How long did you want the place for? *(She takes an inventory from the pigeon-hole.)*

BRUCE. *(shutting the bedroom door)* Oh, any time – how long do you want to let it for?

CECILY. Well, Mavis – my friend – will be away three months at least.

BRUCE. That's all right by me. *(He comes down centre to the drawer on the table.)*

CECILY. *(at the bureau, absorbed with the inventory, so that she is half-turned away from BRUCE)* Will you require plate and linen?

(BRUCE has noticed the newspaper in the drawer on the table. He starts slightly. Perusing it intently, he answers CECILY's questions abstractedly.)

BRUCE. *(fogged)* Plate and linen?

CECILY. Yes.

BRUCE. *(pulling himself together and standing centre)* Well, I suppose I need plates to eat off – but I reckon I can buy them at a store.

CECILY. No – no – I mean silver, knives, forks and spoons.

BRUCE. Oh, yes – please.

CECILY. And linen – sheets and pillow-cases.

BRUCE. Oh, yeh – yeh – yes, please. Oh, yes, rather, I hadn't thought of – *(He breaks off, laughing at himself.)* You must think me no end of a dumb cluck, but you see, I've never taken a flat before.

CECILY. *(smiling)* I rather guessed as much.

BRUCE. I've always wandered about up till now. I left this country when I was seventeen. I went to South Africa first. Then East, Indo China. I got lost there and lived with a savage tribe for six months – very decent, respectable little people, too, except on party nights. I say – I hope I'm not boring you?

CECILY. No, no, do go on. *(crossing left)* Won't you sit down?

(BRUCE sits at right end of the sofa, but then rises in a diffident, boyish kind of way to allow CECILY to sit first, in the armchair left. He is putting on an act of "out-door-man-not-used-to-the-society-of-women." Then he starts off again with:)

BRUCE. After that I was in Japan for a while, but I didn't care for it much.

CECILY. Why?

BRUCE. I dunno; the Japanese didn't seem to me to be – well, they didn't seem to be at all Japanese. After that I drifted over to 'Frisco and the Yukon.

CECILY. I know, where men are men and Dangerous Dan McGrew and all that.

BRUCE. Yea, all that bunk. For the last two years I've been living in a shack by the side of a Canadian river.

CECILY. How thrilling!

BRUCE. Oh, I dunno, bit lonesome; there's nobody to talk to except the beavers and they're far too busy to be good conversationalists. So you see, I must ask you to forgive me if I'm too garrulous now, and not very – er – civilized.

CECILY. Oh, it's a nice change not to be too civilized.

BRUCE. Most women don't think so.

CECILY. Don't they?

BRUCE. No; most women like living soft. They like permanent waves, cinemas and ice-cream-sodas. They hate adventure, or roughing it.

CECILY. Oh, I don't think that's quite true. The trouble is, most women don't get the chance of adventure.

BRUCE. If they did get the chance they'd turn it down.

CECILY. I shouldn't. I know I shouldn't.

BRUCE. No? Well, maybe you're different, in fact I'm sure you are.

(There is a pause.)

CECILY. *(rising and changing the subject)* Well, do you think you'd like to take the place – Mr. – er –

BRUCE. Oh, but of course, I haven't told you my name, have I? Lovell – Bruce Lovell.

CECILY. Thank you.

BRUCE. You see, Miss – now isn't that funny? I don't know your name either.

CECILY. Harrington, Cecily Harrington. I'll give you a –

BRUCE. *(producing a notebook)* No. I'll just make a note of that, if you don't mind.

CECILY. *(smiling)* How very methodical.

BRUCE. *(writing)* Miss Cecily Harrington, H-A-R-R – yes, it's a habit of mine. I'm much more precise than you'd imagine. I think it's the result of living alone so much. You see, if one doesn't do things in their right order, one's liable to get very slovenly living out in the wilds – I don't mean that I dress for dinner, or anything like that – but you've got to keep a hold on yourself.

CECILY. I understand.

BRUCE. You'd be no end amused if you knew some of the things I've got written down here – fr'instance, once a fortnight I've made a note. What d'you think it is?

CECILY. I don't know.

(BRUCE *is still seated.* CECILY *leans over to read the notebook.*)

"Get your hair cut."

(They both laugh.)

Now really, we must be business-like – you do want to take the place, then?

BRUCE. Sure I do. It suits me down to the ground. You see, I haven't any real plans, I just thought I'd take a little place – and look round and decide what I really wanted to do.

CECILY. I see.

BRUCE. You've no idea how exciting it is to be in London again after all these years. Sometimes I didn't believe it would ever happen. But it has. I struck it lucky, and here I am in London with money to burn.

CECILY. It must be rather thrilling.

BRUCE. Well, you know how it is, when you've looked forward to something – when you've planned the things you're going to do.

CECILY. Well, as a matter of fact, I do know. I've done it for years. All the time I've been grinding away in an office, I was always planning what I'd do if I had some money of my own – though I never dreamed I should have – and then, quite suddenly, like a fairy-tale it happened. Mavis, my friend, and I won second prize in a Sweep.

BRUCE. How much did you win?

CECILY. Twenty thousand pounds – ten thousand each.

BRUCE. Gosh! Let me look at you. I've never met anybody who'd won a big Sweep before. I've never believed they were real people somehow… I've always thought they were just a lot of names that were made up in the newspaper offices.

CECILY. Yes, I know what you mean.

BRUCE. Well! Well! Well! If it isn't an impertinence – what are you going to do with it? I mean – are you going to travel, or what?

CECILY. Well, I was supposed to be getting married.

BRUCE. Married? – Oh, I see, yes, to this fiancé you were expecting – (*He pretends to start to get up.*) Here, I'd better scram.

CECILY. Oh, no, it's all right, he can't possibly arrive for another half-hour.

BRUCE. It certainly is terrible the way I go rattling on; but, you know, it's funny, but somehow I find you particularly easy to talk to.

CECILY. Yes, it's strange, but I feel the same way. I think you inspire confidence somehow.

BRUCE. *(elated)* Do you think so? Do you really think so?

(The telephone rings. – CECILY *moves to answer it.)*

CECILY. Excuse me. *(Into the 'phone.)* Hullo… Yes… No, I'm sorry, it's just been let… Thank you. Good-bye. *(She hangs up.)*

BRUCE. Do you mind if I ask you a question?

CECILY. No, go ahead. *(She sits on the downstage arm of the armchair left)*

BRUCE. Why did you say you were *supposed* to be getting married?

CECILY. Because I'm in a state of indecision about it – somehow or other things have changed.

BRUCE. *(simply)* You mean that since you've won this money you want to enjoy a little independence before you settle down?

CECILY. *(gaping at him in astonishment)* But how on earth could you possibly guess that?

BRUCE. I told you I was used to summing people up quickly.

CECILY. *(still breathless)* Yes, but even so…

BRUCE. And then, you see, I found you a particularly interesting subject… from the first moment I saw you.

(There is another pause. CECILY *rises and goes to the table for the cigarette-box.)*

CECILY. Have a cigarette? *(She hands him the cigarette-box.)*

BRUCE. Say, that's a cute idea; fancy making a cigarette-box out of a book.

CECILY. *(moving to the mantelpiece for matches)* There was quite a vogue for them a few years ago – it's rather a nice binding, my fiancé gave it to me.

BRUCE. It's a new one on me. *(He has taken a cigarette and is looking at the title of the book.)* The Arabian Nights… Well, well, well. How that takes me back! I remember as a kid how sorry I was for that poor girl who had to tell all those stories to the Sultan.

CECILY. *(lighting his cigarette for him)* Scheherazade?

BRUCE. Yes, that's the name. *(He replaces the cigarette-box on the table.)*

CECILY. It's a ghastly thought, having to make up a fresh story every night to save your life.

BRUCE. And yet, after all, no worse than being a serial-writer. How long have you been engaged to this—

CECILY. About five years.

BRUCE. When did you see him last?

CECILY. Three years ago, when he was home on leave.

BRUCE. D'you mean to say he was content to be engaged all this time?

CECILY. But, of course.

BRUCE. No "of course" about it. He ought to have whisked you off with him to the Sudan.

CECILY. *(sitting in the armchair left)* But he couldn't, his pay wasn't sufficient. You see, his job is a—

BRUCE. Hell! He could get another job.

CECILY. That's a bit difficult in these days.

BRUCE. Nothing's difficult if you've got sufficient reason for it. There's nothing in the world you can't get if you make up your mind to it... Hanging about for five years – Gosh, it beats me... Why, if I'd been – Well, I should call it half-hearted.

CECILY. Oh, I shouldn't say that – It's almost as though I knew him too well.

BRUCE. Exactly! He's gone stale on you.

CECILY. *(with a smile)* That's not a very nice way of putting it, and yet... oh, I don't know –

(The sunshine outside begins to fade. During the following scene it becomes evident that the sky has clouded over.)

BRUCE. Be honest with yourself, and then you'll be honest with him.

CECILY. I know…

BRUCE. Can I help you?

CECILY. No. *(Her head is still averted.)*

*(***BRUCE*** *puts his cigarette out on the little table in front of the sofa.)*

BRUCE. Look at me a moment.

(She turns to him.)

Are you terribly glad and excited that he's coming back? *(She does not answer.)* No, you're not. Can you possibly be in love with him, then? You may make a mistake now and the real thing may come along too late.

CECILY. *(looking up)* But how can I be sure this isn't the real thing?

BRUCE. *(his gaze is almost hypnotic)* It isn't. You know it isn't – don't you?

*(***CECILY*** *rises.)*

Oh, I understand so well what you're going through; I've been through the same sort of thing.

CECILY. *You* have?

BRUCE. There have been girls I've met, that I've liked plenty, everything's been very – er – suitable, and all that. It could have been all so easy. And yet – all along – I've known that one day – one day, when I least expected it, I would walk into a room and see a girl – and it would be all over – like that. *(He snaps his finger.)*

CECILY. Do you think it can happen like that?

BRUCE. It has happened – today.

(There is a long pause.)

CECILY. You must be mad.

BRUCE. *(rising)* I know it looks like it – I hadn't got time to take the usual line – situated as you are, you may commit yourself at any minute. I had to speak at once, even at the risk of appearing crazy to you.

CECILY. But... but half an hour ago I had never met you.

BRUCE. *(simply)* I know, that's what's so wonderful.

CECILY. *(desperately)* These things don't happen.

BRUCE. They do. You have happened – to me. You know that. *(After a pause.)* You do know it – don't you?

CECILY. *(turning slightly upstage towards the mantelpiece)* It isn't possible.

BRUCE. *(touching her arm and turning her back – very gently)* From the very first moment that I saw you as you turned round from the mantelpiece, I knew. I could see everything in your eyes. You thought for a moment I was your fiancé, your feelings showed so clearly the desire for escape, the unhappiness at hurting someone who cares for you, and beneath it all your craving for life and adventure calling to mine.

(She turns away from him to the mantelpiece again.)

You believe me?

CECILY. Yes, I do believe you.

(He turns away with a sigh of relief. He opens the dining-room door and stands looking in, presumably at the picture.)

BRUCE. This isn't going to end here, you know.

CECILY. It must.

BRUCE. It can't. I'm going to see you again... soon... today.

CECILY. Out of the question.

BRUCE. Come and lunch with me now.

CECILY. It's no use talking like this.

BRUCE. You can write a note for him.

CECILY. I've done that already.

BRUCE. You have? Well, then –

CECILY. It would be cruel.

BRUCE. Half-measures are fatal.

CECILY. I must risk that.

(There is another pause. BRUCE comes to a decision. He crosses to the chair up right for his hat and mackintosh.)

BRUCE. All right, I give in – for the moment – but I tell you what I'll do. I'm going to the Savoy Grill. I shall wait for you in the vestibule till – what's the time now? – ten to one – till three o'clock.

CECILY. They'll have you turned out for loitering or something.

BRUCE. I should worry. Will you – in the event of things not being O.K. with your fiancé – will you promise to come and join me?

CECILY. But why?

BRUCE. You don't actually dislike me, do you?

(She hesitates. His frankness compels her.)

CECILY. *(half-laughing)* No.

BRUCE. If there wasn't somebody else I might stand some sort of a chance?

CECILY. I – I don't know. You're a very impulsive creature.

BRUCE. So are you at heart, but you've never had the chance to give way to it.

CECILY. *(wandering over right)* No, that's true.

BRUCE. Anyway, I want you to get to know me better, and lunch is as good a way as any – you'll be able to make sure that I don't eat peas with a knife or insult the waiters. We could go for a walk in the park afterwards, it's a lovely day.

CECILY. *(looking out of the window)* It's clouded over.

BRUCE. It's only a shower, you'll see!

CECILY. *(laughing)* Persuasion is your strong point, isn't it?

(He sighs.)

BRUCE. Well, I shall have to leave it at that. If things don't pan out all right with this fellow, you'll come?

CECILY. No – no, at least – I can't promise.

BRUCE. *(quietly, as he crosses to the door)* You'll be along all right.

CECILY. *(firmly)* Good-bye.

BRUCE. *(shaking his head, with a smile)* Au revoir.

(He turns and exits quickly.)

*(**CECILY** is left staring after him. When his personality has quite faded from the room, she gives a little gasp.)*

CECILY. Well, really!!

*(She turns away thoughtfully and drifts unconsciously to the dining-room door, which is open; she looks up and catches sight of the picture, and smiles ruminatively. She looks back at the door through which **BRUCE** has gone, and then at the picture again. She shuts the dining-room door decisively.)*

Oh, no, no, no! It's too silly!

(She goes to the mantelpiece, lakes the note and tears it into pieces.)

(The telephone bell rings.)

(answering it, kneeling on the armchair left) Hullo? Hullo? Yes?... Who is it?... Nigel! Where are you speaking from?... Tilbury?... Only just what?... Oh, through the Customs – good. How long will you be?... About an hour. Yes, dear, lovely... Good-bye... What?... What mood?... Oh no, my dear, that wasn't a mood. I meant it... You will postpone the wedding – please... No, let's get it clear now; perhaps it's easier over the 'phone... If I wait till I see you it'll make it – ... Oh, Nigel, I have thought, but I said it all in my last letter, and I feel just the same. *(Her voice is becoming tremulous.)* Yes, I know, dear, it *is* horrid... but it isn't entirely selfishness... I know things have been very difficult for you out there, but they've been pretty hard for me at the office. I... But, Nigel, I'm only asking you to postpone – *(Something that he says turns her voice flat and toneless.)*

Oh, I'm sorry… I'm sorry you feel like that about it… Is that your final word?… Nigel, how can you say things like that!… *(She is in tears by now.)* One moment, Nigel, listen, please… perhaps if we –

(He has rung off.) Nigel? Hullo? Nigel? – Oh!

(curtain)

Scene II

(Scene – The same. Two hours later.)

(NIGEL is seated on the sofa, CECILY's note in his hand. MAVIS is in the armchair left.)

(NIGEL is what is known as a "typical Englishman." A neat, almost military head, clipped moustache, and, the skin stretched tightly over a sharp-boned face. Fever has made his tan slightly jaundiced, and has exaggerated the size of his dark eyes which, at the moment, are stricken and piteous.)

(For a while there is silence.)

NIGEL. I'm sorry to make such an ass of myself, but it's been a bit of a shock – I mean, on top of the excitement of coming back.

MAVIS. I know.

NIGEL. I can't believe it... Cecily... What am I going to do, Mavis? – What *am* I going to do?... I mean, it was everything, all my work... the whole reason.

MAVIS. What can I say? How can I – ?

NIGEL. I wish I hadn't been so impatient with her on the 'phone. God, if I'd realized!

MAVIS. I simply can't understand where she's gone.

NIGEL. What's the time now? Three o'clock. I never dreamed it was as serious as this. *(He reads the note for the tenth time and laughs sharply and bitterly.)* "P.S. Your ring has gone to the cleaners, you shall have it as soon as it comes back." – She's thought of everything, hasn't she?

MAVIS. If only she'd talked to me more about it, but she's been bottling it up inside her for weeks, it was only this morning, as I told you, that she really laid her cards on the table.

NIGEL. *(reading)* "I'm sorry, I can't go through with it, please don't wait for me – there's nothing to be gained by it. I'm terribly sorry, but one must be honest." It's this stinking, filthy money – damn and blast it!

MAVIS. *(half to herself)* "The root of all evil," as Auntie Loo-Loo would say. Aren't some of these old clichés sickeningly right on occasions? Like some frightful old bore saying: "I told you so"; and talking of old bores, thank heavens it was I who found you waiting outside instead of Auntie Loo-Loo.

(She is talking for the sake of talk. He isn't listening.)

NIGEL. What?

MAVIS. *(rising)* Look here – do you think it's wise to stay? – I mean, we've no idea when Cecily will be back.

NIGEL. *(grimly)* I'll wait – a week if necessary.

MAVIS. Auntie Loo-Loo might be back before Cecily – it'll all have to be explained – it'll be ghastly for you.

NIGEL. Nothing can be worse than this – I'm going to wait and see her.

MAVIS. Really, I'm afraid…

NIGEL. *(in an outburst – rising)* Good God! What do you think I'm made of? Do you think I'm going to sit back and do nothing? *(moving away to the window)* No, by hell! I'm going to make a fight for it.

MAVIS. *(in spite of herself)* Ah, that's better.

NIGEL. *(looking moodily out of the window)* All this time, out in that bloody place, lying there in a muck sweat, night after night, I dreamed of today – It's funny, isn't it? – the things I've given up, for nothing – nothing!

MAVIS. *(helplessly)* Oh, Nigel.

NIGEL. Sorry, Mavis. This is a poor show for you… don't you worry about me, old girl, you go out. It's a lovely day – at least, it seemed it when I landed… To think it was less than three hours ago. I shall be all right, honestly.

MAVIS. *(moving to right end of sofa)* Well, if you'd rather I left – ?

NIGEL. Oh, no, no, it isn't that.

MAVIS. Then I'll stay. *(She sits on the right arm of the sofa.)*

NIGEL. It's damn good of you. But I'm not much fun this afternoon. Rather "The Wreck of the Hesperus." Never mind, we'll get things straight, somehow; I shall be able to laugh her out of it – we've always had the same sense of humour. I can't see anything particularly funny in it at the moment, but I dare say it'll come.

(AUNTIE LOO-LOO is heard offstage. NIGEL crosses to below the sofa.)

AUNTIE LOO-LOO. *(off)* Children! Children!

MAVIS. *(rising and crossing to the window-seat)* Oh, Lord! Nothing funny about that! *(She leaves her gloves on the window-seat.)*

(AUNTIE LOO-LOO bursts into the room. She concentrates on NIGEL, so does not notice CECILY's absence.)

AUNTIE LOO-LOO. Nigel! At last! Let me take a good look at you – oh, but how well you're looking! Perhaps a teeny bit greyer round the temples, but it suits you, and what does a little grey hair matter when you're as happy as you are? How are you? Splendid? Good! I never saw you looking so debonair and gay – and darling Cecily's been bubbling over with excitement, haven't you, Cec – ? *(Looking round.)* Oh, but – but where is she?

(MAVIS takes her hat off, leaves it on the bureau, and moves round in front of the bureau chair.)

I was so absorbed in you, Nigel, that I thought Mavis was Cecily; aren't I a silly!

(She laughs affectedly, then becomes aware of the stony faces of NIGEL and MAVIS.)

But where *is* Cecily?

(There is complete silence.)

Is anything wrong?

MAVIS. Everything's wrong, Miss Garrard. Cecily's gone out. She wasn't here when Nigel arrived—

AUNTIE LOO-LOO. Wasn't here when—?

MAVIS. She's broken off the engagement.

AUNTIE LOO-LOO. Cecily?… I don't believe it.

(For answer, **NIGEL** *hands her* **CECILY***'s note.* **AUNTIE LOO-LOO** *sits on the sofa, puts her bag beside her and reads the note with growing dismay.)*

Oh, but she can't do it! She can't – where is she? I don't understand. Why on earth should she? – I mean – why?

NIGEL. *(more to himself than to her)* She wrote to me a couple of months ago, asking me to postpone the wedding.

AUNTIE LOO-LOO. *Postpone* the wedding – after all these years of waiting – ?

NIGEL. Yes, that's just what I thought –

AUNTIE LOO-LOO. But the dear girl's been dancing all over the room this morning at the thought of you coming back!

MAVIS. *(moving forward to centre)* We shan't help Nigel by deceiving him, Miss Garrard.

AUNTIE LOO-LOO. I'm sure I shouldn't dream of –

MAVIS. *(moving away to the window)* The trouble is, we've none of us taken her sufficiently seriously.

(There is a thoughtful pause.)

AUNTIE LOO-LOO. And yet, you know, she hasn't talked about him… as far as I've been able to see, she hasn't had any letters from him, and I'm sure he hasn't 'phoned – at least, not while I –

NIGEL. Who?

AUNTIE LOO-LOO. The other man – whoever he is.

MAVIS. Oh, no, no, no, of that I'm absolutely certain. There's no question of another man.

NIGEL. Are you sure?

MAVIS. Positive.

AUNTIE LOO-LOO. Rubbish! Why should any girl give up a man unless she is quite certain of another one?

MAVIS. *(to* NIGEL*)* You can take it from me, quite definitely, there isn't anybody else.

NIGEL. Then there may be some slight chance for me?

AUNTIE LOO-LOO. Of course there is! – She must be talked to, be made to see reason; girls can't do things like that – I mean, to write a note like this. *(She is reading it again.)* And in any case, why hasn't her ring returned from the cleaners? I went in yesterday most particularly, and they promised it before twelve this morning without fail.

(MAVIS gives a stifled shriek of hysteria and buries her face in her hands.)

My dear Mavis, whatever's the matter with you?

(CECILY enters. She is looking flushed and her eyes are shining – she checks herself as she sees NIGEL. AUNTIE LOO-LOO rises and stands in the angle made by the sofa and the table. MAVIS moves down to the bureau chair. NIGEL is in front of the fireplace.)

CECILY. *(just inside the door, which she has shut)* Oh, Nigel! I asked you not to wait, dear. It would have been so much better not to.

NIGEL. I had to.

CECILY. I'm so terribly sorry – I did so want to spare you this, but there's nothing you can do – *really!*

AUNTIE LOO-LOO. What a welcome! – All the way from the Sudan!

CECILY. Yes, I know. Nigel, I'm hating myself, but –

AUNTIE LOO-LOO. If you won't kiss him, you might at least shake hands.

MAVIS. Don't you think, Miss Garrard, it would be better if we left them together for a bit?

CECILY. No, no, Mavis – I'd rather you didn't go. I can only stay a moment – I've just come in for some thicker shoes.

(MAVIS sits on the arm of the bureau chair.)

AUNTIE LOO-LOO. Thicker shoes? What for?

CECILY. *(coming to the back of the sofa and facing* **NIGEL** *across it)* It's better for us both if you don't go. Nigel, if there was anything to do to make it easier I'd do it, but there isn't.

*(***CECILY**'s *manner is changed; her calmness, which is not at all callous, seems to be sustained by some inward light of happiness.)*

NIGEL. Cecily, listen.

CECILY. Nigel, I can't –

NIGEL. If it really means so much to you I'm willing to postpone the wedding.

AUNTIE LOO-LOO. There now! He can't say fairer than that.

CECILY. I'm sorry, but it's too late.

NIGEL. You mean after what I said on the 'phone this morning? I'm sorry, Cecily, but really –

CECILY. Oh, no, no, it was perfectly reasonable of you to be furious; it isn't because of that at all.

NIGEL. What then?

CECILY. *(at a loss)* It's… it's just too late, that's all.

AUNTIE LOO-LOO. *(moving round the table to* **CECILY***)* Really, Cecily, how can you be so irritating to write a letter like this, and go on saying "it's just too late" like that.

CECILY. *(impatiently)* Please, Auntie Loo-Loo!

MAVIS. *(sitting in the bureau chair)* It's no good, Cecily – Auntie Loo-Loo's right – for once. Nigel's given in most generously and you refuse to meet him – you must give him some reason.

AUNTIE LOO-LOO. I should think so indeed.

NIGEL. Is there another man, Cecily?

CECILY. There wasn't.

MAVIS. There *wasn't?*

AUNTIE LOO-LOO. But there is now? I knew it all along.

CECILY. You're wrong, Auntie Loo-Loo. I only met him this morning after you and Mavis had gone out.

NIGEL. *How* long did you say you've known him?

CECILY. Since this morning – oh, I know it sounds absurd, but –

NIGEL. Absurd! How long was he here?

CECILY. Oh, I don't know... half an hour or so.

NIGEL. But d'you mean to say that this man – who you've only seen once for half an hour – ?

CECILY. I've seen him again since he was here – I've just had lunch with him.

AUNTIE LOO-LOO. Cecily, how could you! How *common!* *(After a slight pause.)* Where?

CECILY. At the Savoy.

AUNTIE LOO-LOO. Oh! *(She says this as if the Savoy made it slightly better.)*

NIGEL. *(moving down stage)* Who is the man, anyway?

CECILY. His name's Bruce Lovell.

MAVIS. When are you seeing him again?

CECILY. Well, he's waiting for me outside in a taxi – we're going down to Kew.

MAVIS. Ah! "Kew in the Spring" – I see.

AUNTIE LOO-LOO. So *that's* why you wanted to change your shoes.

NIGEL. *(moving up to the fireplace)* You're not going to marry him?

CECILY. He's asked me to.

NIGEL. *(angrily)* Really?

AUNTIE LOO-LOO. Well, anyway, he won't be taking this flat.

CECILY. *(smiling)* No, I'm afraid not.

AUNTIE LOO-LOO. *(moving down to MAVIS at the bureau chair)* Well, we must hope for the best. Thank heavens I've placed the flat in Harrods' hands now. They've promised to send someone along this afternoon.

NIGEL. *(furiously, moving down and standing below the armchair left)* What the hell does the flat matter, or anything else? This is my whole life smashed to bits – isn't there anything we can do to stop her?

AUNTIE LOO-LOO. *(turning to* **NIGEL***)* I'm sure I don't know, it's no good attacking me.

NIGEL. It's too ludicrous to talk about marrying a man you've only just met.

CECILY. I may not marry him at all, Nigel – but – oh, it's been so exciting giving way to an impulse. We're all impulsive at heart, but most of us never get the chance to indulge it.

MAVIS. *(quietly)* Did *he* say that?

CECILY. *(glancing at her sharply)* How did you know?

MAVIS. *(facetiously)* My gipsy blood, dear. By the way, did he know about your share in the Sweep?

CECILY. Ah! I knew that was coming. – Yes, I did tell him.

AUNTIE LOO-LOO. Oh, well, of course –

CECILY. But that has nothing to do with it – he's got plenty of his own – he made it in Canada.

MAVIS. Oh – "The wide open spaces," of course that *would* get you in your present state.

AUNTIE LOO-LOO. *(drifting across to* **NIGEL***)* I think it's too disgraceful. Here have I been slaving myself to the bone all the morning – had a filthy lunch – and now –

NIGEL. *(taking no notice of* **AUNTIE LOO-LOO***)* Of all the damnably inconsiderate and selfish things –

AUNTIE LOO-LOO. *(turning her back on* **NIGEL** *and speaking to* **MAVIS** *and* **CECILY***)* Besides, think what people will say!

NIGEL. *(very violently)* Oh, shut up!

AUNTIE LOO-LOO. *(swinging round on* **NIGEL***)* Really, that's no way to talk!

*(***MAVIS** *rises and crosses to them.)*

If you're going to turn on me just when –

MAVIS. Miss Garrard, it's no use quarrelling with Nigel –

AUNTIE LOO-LOO. Be quiet! You aren't even one of the family.

(The front-door bell rings.)

Ah, that'll be the person from Harrods. *(To* NIGEL.*)* Here, take your letter.

(She hurries offstage.)

MAVIS. *(moving away to the window)* They would send someone in the middle of all this, of course.

AUNTIE LOO-LOO. *(the soul of charm, offstage)* Oh, do come up. I'm afraid it's rather a long way, but it's nice and airy when you get to the top. *(coming in – aside)* Such a nice man! Now this – this is the sitting-room!

*(*BRUCE *enters.)*

BRUCE. *(to* CECILY*)* I'm awfully sorry, I got kind of tired waiting in the taxi –

CECILY. Bruce, you shouldn't have –

AUNTIE LOO-LOO. *(puzzled)* Bruce?

MAVIS. Are you Bruce Lovell?

BRUCE. That's me.

NIGEL. What the Hell!

AUNTIE LOO-LOO. *(left of* BRUCE, *by the door up right centre)* But who? – D'you mean to say that – ? I thought Harrods – How dare you! How dare you set foot in this flat?

CECILY. Auntie Loo-Loo!

AUNTIE LOO-LOO. Be quiet, Cecily! I must deal with this! *(to* BRUCE*)* I'd have you know that I am Cecily's only relation and as such her guardian, and I insist – I have the right to insist – upon an explanation.

BRUCE. An explanation of what, er – er – Miss Harrington?

AUNTIE LOO-LOO. My name is Garrard. Here's this poor boy come all the way from the Sudan to find himself jilted –

*(*BRUCE *sees* NIGEL *and moves towards him.)*

There's no other word for it – jilted, by my niece – and it's all your fault.

MAVIS. *(moving up to* AUNTIE LOO-LOO*)* Please, Miss Garrard!

AUNTIE LOO-LOO. It's no good, leave me alone, and don't interfere –

(She catches BRUCE*'s arm and turns him. They are standing centre)*

Who are you? What are you? Who are your people? The only Lovells I ever knew were the Shropshire Lovells who drank!

BRUCE. Miss Garrard, please believe me, I do understand your anxiety.

AUNTIE LOO-LOO. Hold your tongue!

CECILY. Really, this is too much. Mavis, take her away.

AUNTIE LOO-LOO. If there's anything to be said it's for –

NIGEL. If there's anything to be said I think I'd better say it.

MAVIS. Nigel's quite right, Miss Garrard, it would be much better if we went. We'll go for a little walk.

AUNTIE LOO-LOO. Walk! After I've been subjected to this revolting scene?

MAVIS. Very well, then, we'll take a taxi and go and have tea somewhere.

AUNTIE LOO-LOO. Tea! I couldn't touch it.

MAVIS. *(fetching her hat from the bureau and putting it on in front of the mirror over the bureau)* I'll take you to Gunter's.

AUNTIE LOO-LOO. *(considering)* Well – Very well, then, but under protest.

*(*MAVIS *fetches her gloves from the window-seat.)*

(to CECILY*)* You've disgraced your mother's name – if your poor dear father had been alive things might have been very different – however, I've done my best – one can't do more. Well, you've made your bed and you'll have to –

(She becomes confused over what she has said, and exits quickly.)

MAVIS. *(advancing a step or two back into the room)* All I've got to say, Cecily, is that – *(She pauses, confronting* BRUCE *and looking at him with no apparent friendliness)* – but no, perhaps this isn't the moment.

(**MAVIS** *exits.*)

NIGEL. Well, thank God she's got rid of your Aunt.

(*Re-enter* **AUNTIE LOO-LOO,** *annoyed at spoiling her exit.*)

AUNTIE LOO-LOO. My bag!

(*She moves down stage with extreme dignity, collects her bag from the sofa and exits again in stony silence.*)

NIGEL. (*coming up to* **BRUCE**) Now, look here, Lovell, you've gathered by now, if you didn't know before, who I am.

BRUCE. I have, and I want to tell you here and now that I'm sorry – not sorry for what I've done, but because I realize that you must be feeling pretty sore.

NIGEL. You know, do you, that we've been engaged for a long time?

BRUCE. Too long a time. She was asking you for a postponement before she met me.

CECILY. You know that's true, Nigel.

NIGEL. Yes, but now I've agreed to the postponement.

CECILY. But you see – since then –

BRUCE. See here, this discussion isn't going to do anybody any good – except the taxi-driver ticking up outside.

NIGEL. You can say what you like – I'm going to have this out here and now.

BRUCE. It rests between you and Cecily. My position, to say the least of it, is embarrassing. We'd arranged to go to Kew and as far as I'm concerned it's still on. How about you, Cecily?

(**CECILY** *nods.*)

I admit you're entitled to your say. I'm darned if I'm going to sit in that draughty taxi any longer, so if you'll excuse me I'll go and wait in the dining-room – there's a picture there that rather fascinates me.

(He exits left into the dining-room.)

NIGEL. *(frantically)* For God's sake, Cecily – you can't do this – think what you're doing!

CECILY. *(with quiet sincerity)* My dear, I have thought – I've thought of nothing else for weeks.

NIGEL. I suppose a woman gets a kick out of a couple of men fighting over her.

CECILY. Nigel! What's the use of talking like that!

NIGEL. But think, Cecily, think how well we've always got on together – the grand times we've had – the understanding – we've been so terribly fond of each other.

CECILY. But, Nigel, I still *am* fond of you. My feelings haven't changed for you, it's just that I've found out they're not strong enough.

NIGEL. *(sitting down on the sofa)* I see exactly what has happened. I've been a "standby" – an escape from your office; now you've got your money you don't need me.

CECILY. *(by right arm of sofa)* You're entitled to think that. I thought for one awful moment this morning that it might be, but I know now my feelings for you were – and are – perfectly genuine; it's just that something stronger has come into my life. I may have lost my head – it may come to nothing – but there it is.

(There is a thoughtful pause, finally broken by NIGEL.)

NIGEL. All right. I'm not going to bother you any more now. I don't say I shan't try to influence you during the next few weeks – I shall. I shall do my damnedest, but I can see it's no use at the moment, besides I only lose my head and say bitter things and I can't bear doing that because, whatever happens, whatever you may do, I love you – and I always shall. *(He rises and there is a slight pause.)* I mean that, don't forget.

(He strides across to the door up right centre and exits. CECILY watches him, genuinely moved, then sits on the

sofa, crying a little. After a pause **BRUCE** *enters. He regards her for a second as he closes the door.)*

BRUCE. *(moving over to the window)* I'm afraid it's been a bit tough for you – I'm sorry.

CECILY. *(rising – quite recovered)* Come on – let's go to Kew.

BRUCE. We shall have to hurry if we're to get any time there.

CECILY. Right! I'll just change my shoes – I won't be a moment.

(She exits into the bedroom up left centre. **BRUCE** *crosses deliberately to the small drawer, which has been placed on the floor downstage right by the bureau during the quick change of the previous scene, and takes out the piece of newspaper. He reads it intently for a moment and chuckles to himself.* **CECILY** *returns and* **BRUCE**, *unnoticed, hides the paper behind his back.)*

Hullo! What are you doing?

BRUCE. Just fastening my shoe. Shall we go?

CECILY. Yes. I'm ready.

(He holds the door open for her and she passes out in front of him. He pauses a moment, wondering how to get rid of the piece of newspaper, then stuffs the paper into his pocket and follows her)

(curtain)

ACT TWO

Scene I

(Scene – The interior of a very charming country cottage. About 11 o'clock on a sunny April morning.)

(The room is timbered, but it is not tiresomely "ye olde" and you don't bang your head if you wish to stand upright. Through the French windows is a glimpse of an enchanting garden.)

(The cottage is, in fact, a converted inn. To one side is a rather "quaint" staircase leading down to a cellar. Another staircase leads upstairs. A door, left, up two steps leads to the kitchen, and the front door up right opens straight into the garden.)

(The room is in the middle of being "put straight." The trunk which we have seen in CECILY*'s flat is there, centre by the fireplace, and there is a pair of steps standing near one of the windows. There is a low sofa right. A japanned tropical box is in front of the table left centre)*

(See property plot.)

(The curtain rises on an empty stage. BRUCE *and* CECILY *can be heard outside the front door, talking and laughing. There is the sound of a key in the lock.)*

BRUCE. Can you manage? Sure that lock's not too stiff?

CECILY. No, it's all right.

*(*CECILY *enters and puts the key on the inside of the door.* BRUCE *is seen in the doorway.)*

(Crossing left) I'll just put these parcels in the kitchen.

*(She exits into the kitchen. **BRUCE** draws back the curtains and opens the French windows. **CECILY** returns.)*

Oh, isn't it heavenly!

(They embrace passionately, right centre)

The peace!

BRUCE. *(sitting on the right arm of the sofa)* What did I tell you?

CECILY. *(kneeling beside him on the sofa)* Yes, I know – it was only that I thought it might be a bit inaccessible.

BRUCE. Well, isn't it worth it? Not to have neighbours with their chickens and radio and...

CECILY. Of course it is. As long as you don't complain when you have to walk three miles to buy a packet of cigarettes.

BRUCE. Even that will be worth it.

CECILY. I shall never let you leave me for a minute. Don't you think we're silly not to have the telephone?

BRUCE. Of course not. That's the whole point of living in the country – no telephones, no cars – the Simple Life.

CECILY. Yes – and in any case I've got Don for protection.

BRUCE. And me! Do you know what today is?

CECILY. Yes, Tuesday.

BRUCE. No, don't be silly – don't you realize –

CECILY. Darling, of course. *(She kisses him again.)*

(They both laugh.)

BRUCE. Do you remember saying these things don't happen?

CECILY. It seems incredible, doesn't it, that it was only six weeks ago.

BRUCE. Since then we've been married, we've had this glorious honeymoon, we've found our cottage, and here we are.

CECILY. Of course, Auntie Loo-Loo would say I had thrown myself at your head!

BRUCE. And Auntie Loo-Loo would be quite wrong. You know perfectly well if I'd had my way I'd have married you that afternoon, instead of going to Kew.

CECILY. Yes, I do believe you would.

BRUCE. I certainly would. *(Noticing japanned box.)* Aw hell! *(He rises and crosses to the box.)* I didn't know I'd left this up here yesterday. I'll take it down to the dark room now.

CECILY. *(rising)* Cellar, dear.

BRUCE. It's going to be my dark room, so it may as well get used to being called it.

CECILY. What's in it, dear?

BRUCE. *(starting to haul the box towards the stairs leading to the cellar)* Just a lot of my photographic junk. One moment, there's something in here you might like.

CECILY. Amongst the photographic junk? You've always been so mysterious about that box – now we shall see.

(BRUCE produces a Chinese shawl.)

Where did it come from?

BRUCE. *(taking the shawl over to her by the sofa)* Oh, from a man – in Hankow I think it was.

CECILY. It's perfectly lovely, darling – thank you.

BRUCE. *(looking out through the French window)* Aah! The estate.

CECILY. *(joining him and standing up stage of him at the window)* Garden, dear.

BRUCE. Oh, no, there's an orchard as well – it's an estate.

CECILY. I do wish I didn't keep worrying about the price, darling. You don't think one thousand five hundred was too much for it? *(She puts the shawl on the table behind the sofa.)*

BRUCE. *(quite casually)* Lord, no! Think of the awful places we looked at, at twice the price.

CECILY. It was the nicest way of spending our honeymoon, wasn't it?

BRUCE. I was afraid you might be disappointed at not going abroad at once.

CECILY. No, I think it's a lovely idea going away when the summer's over.

BRUCE. Yes, that lane would be pretty impassable in the winter, I should think. Oh, my dear, the places I'll show you... Oh, there's that old man the agent told us about – he's working today.

CECILY. Oh, yes; Hodgson. He's evidently got over his "rheumatics." Who's that girl with him, I wonder?

BRUCE. Do gardeners usually bring their girl-friends with them?

CECILY. I'm sure I don't know. (calling out of the window) Good morning, Hodgson!

HODGSON. (off) Good morning, mum!

CECILY. (moving away from the window and speaking urgently) He's coming in. Do you know anything about gardening?

BRUCE. (moving slightly up stage and centre) Not much, do you?

CECILY. Not a thing – we shall have to pretend to be experts.

(HODGSON appears in the window. He is an elderly man, with a funny, direct manner, very matter-of-fact. He is an intensely real person, not at all a piece of theatrical "Mummerset.")

HODGSON. Good morning, mum. Good morning, sir. Sorry to have been away when you've been here before, but my rheumatics have been that bad and old Doctor Gribble said I wasn't to do any work for a few days.

CECILY. Yes, the agent told us.

HODGSON. So I'll make up for lost time now, if you're agreeable. I've always looked after this garden. Mr.

Dunning, what was here before, kept me on even when the house was empty.

BRUCE. Yes, we've had very good accounts of you.

HODGSON. Then, I can stay on?

CECILY. Yes, please, Hodgson.

HODGSON. I was wondering if you'd be wanting someone to look after the house, like.

CECILY. Well, as a matter-of-fact, we haven't fixed anyone yet.

HODGSON. Because there's my niece – Ethel. She hasn't been in service before, but she's a good girl. I brought her along with me in case you would like to see her.

CECILY. Thank you very much, Hodgson, ask her to come in.

HODGSON. *(calling from the window)* Ethel! Come 'ere! *(To* CECILY.*)* She's not very smart, mum, but she's had good schooling – piano lessons and all – and she's willing –

BRUCE. *(to* CECILY*)* Well, you'd be able to – er – coach her.

CECILY. Train her, dear – yes, quite possibly.

(ETHEL enters, she is not particularly bright, and is very untidy, but she looks clean and grins a great deal. She stands downstage of the window, beside HODGSON.)

Good morning, Ethel.

ETHEL. Good morning, miss – er – *(she sees BRUCE)* – mum.

(There is a pause. HODGSON pushes ETHEL centre)

CECILY. Your uncle tells me you might – er – that you want to go into service.

ETHEL. That's right. You see Mum doesn't want me at 'ome any more 'cos my sister Nellie's left school now and there's no need for the two of us...

CECILY. Well, would you like to come and work here?

ETHEL. Yes, please – mum – if you don't mind. I've always done lots of housework at 'ome like, so I'm used to it –

CECILY. Can you cook?

ETHEL. I can make nice milk puddin's and stews and dumplin's and things, but nothing fancy.

(**BRUCE** *has seated himself on the trunk by the fireplace.*)

CECILY. Yes, well, I think we might get on very well. Now what wages would you – er – ?

HODGSON. Well, we'll leave that to you, miss.

CECILY. When can you start?

ETHEL. *(promptly taking off her coat)* Now! Only I 'aven't got an apron on.

HODGSON. 'Ere, you must tell the lady what yer mother said.

CECILY. What was that?

ETHEL. Well, if you please, mum, Mother said I wasn't to sleep in, because, you see, she's all…

HODGSON. On account of leaving her Mum alone. But she could stay as late as you like, mum.

CECILY. Very well, then, that'll be all right. Perhaps you could start straightening up the kitchen.

ETHEL. Oh, yes, mum, I could do that. *(She makes a dive towards the kitchen.)*

CECILY. Oh, these steps, we've finished with them.

(**ETHEL** *dives back to steps, which are against the wall between the small window and the front door, and exits with them into the kitchen.*)

BRUCE. Well, she's got energy, I'll say that for her.

HODGSON. Oh, she's not a bad girl. They've never 'ad a maid sleep in, not all the time I've been working 'ere – since Mr. Dunning converted the place before the war.

CECILY. Converted it from what?

HODGSON. Well, it used to be an inn about fifty years ago.

BRUCE. I thought so.

HODGSON. This 'ere grass track used to be a road, but when they built the new road it fell out of use – became overgrown-like. I don't know, a little bit of grass wouldn't keep me away from no pub.

(They all laugh.)

Well, I'll be getting on with my job. You can see the
weeds growing this spring weather – proper growing
weather it be.

(He exits.)

CECILY. Well, fancy it being an inn. *(calling after him)* Will
you pick some of that lilac – the white and the mauve.

*(BRUCE rises and goes to the table left centre, takes
documents and a fountain-pen from his pocket and sits
at the table.)*

HODGSON. *(off)* Very good, mum.

CECILY. I'll get that trunk unpacked. *(She opens the trunk
and takes out two cushions, which she puts at each end of
the sofa.)* There! That's better already. We needn't have
fresh covers for them if we're going away; we can have
them new next year.

BRUCE. There's a careful girl. Oh, yes, before you do
anything else, dear, I shall want your signature to a
couple of documents.

CECILY. What are they?

BRUCE. Just the last bit of legal tomfoolery in connection
with the purchase of this place.

CECILY. The law does require a lot of fiddling formalities,
doesn't it?

BRUCE. Yes, I'm sorry you've been bothered with it all.
Once the Bank puts my draft through – God knows
what all the delay's about – !

CECILY. *(coming to below him)* Oh, my dear, you know I don't
mind. *(Taking papers.)* Where? Here?

BRUCE. *(handing her a fountain-pen)* Yes. Aren't you going to
read it?

CECILY. *(taking the pen)* Wherein as much heretofore – Do
you mind if I don't?

BRUCE. Not if you don't want to, you unbusinesslike girl.

CECILY. My dear, I used to be businesslike – do I have to put the date?

BRUCE. Yes.

CECILY. *(doing so)* Far too businesslike.

(**BRUCE** *removes the first document and spreads the second before her, his hand over the main part of it.*)

BRUCE. And here.

(**CECILY** *signs it absent-mindedly.*)

CECILY. I'm doing my best to forget all that now.

BRUCE. Are you succeeding?

CECILY. What do you think?

(**BRUCE** *rises, very relieved at having got the papers signed.*)

BRUCE. *(taking her in his arms)* I think that this is just about the most wonderful moment of my life – you and I in our little house – alone –

(**AUNTIE LOO-LOO**'s *head appears round the door.*)

AUNTIE LOO-LOO. Aha! I've caught you!

(They start violently and break apart.)

BRUCE. Aw – hell! – hello!

CECILY. *(running towards her)* Auntie Loo-Loo!

AUNTIE LOO-LOO. *(coming down and meeting her centre)* Just a little surprise, my dear! *(She kisses her.)* I'm afraid my nose is rather cold. I've been meaning to come ever since I got your letter to tell me that you'd found this little nest. Then I discovered that today there was a cheap ticket. Cecily! How well you're looking – radiant! Aren't you proud of her – er – Bruce?

BRUCE. You bet your life!

AUNTIE LOO-LOO. *(moving down to* **BRUCE***)* Yes, only nine shillings return, and such a comfortable train – a corridor. But I must say I think that seven-and-six is an exorbitant charge for the taxi from the station, nearly as much as the whole distance from London – a scandal! Isn't there anyone one could write to?

BRUCE. No one I'm afraid – except the driver.

AUNTIE LOO-LOO. Oh, but he's coming to fetch me. If I don't catch the three-fifteen I shall have to pay another eight-and-tenpence on my ticket and that would never do!

CECILY. Well, do sit down, you must be tired after that journey.

AUNTIE LOO-LOO. (*sitting in the armchair centre and putting a gardening book she has been carrying on the table beside her*) Oh, no, I'm *never* tired – and then, I've got the most wonderful maid for you – she's a Plymouth Sister, I'm afraid, but perhaps that's all to the good these days – at least you know what you're getting.

(ETHEL *enters from the kitchen left.*)

ETHEL. Look! Here's a whopping big parcel – Carrier just left it – feels like books! (*She dumps a large parcel on the japanned box.*)

CECILY. Thank you, Ethel. Oh, just take that box down to the cellar, will you?

(ETHEL *moves the books to the table.*)

BRUCE. No, my dear, I'll see to that. I don't want anyone nosing down there. Let's have it quite clear – it's going to be my private sanctum.

CECILY. Very well.

(*There is a pause as* ETHEL *gapes at* AUNTIE LOO-LOO.)

That's all right, Ethel, you can go. (*As* ETHEL *takes no notice.*) You can go!

(ETHEL *exits into the kitchen.* AUNTIE LOO-LOO's *eyes are on stalks as she watches* ETHEL *out of the room. She turns inquiringly to* CECILY.)

It's awfully kind of you, Auntie Loo-Loo, but you see, I've just engaged that girl.

(BRUCE, *standing left of the table, starts to unpack the books.*)

AUNTIE LOO-LOO. Are you sure you're wise? Have you taken up her references?

CECILY. Oh, that's quite all right – she's the gardener's niece.

AUNTIE LOO-LOO. That may be what he calls her.

BRUCE. *(opening the parcel of books)* It's hard to imagine her anything else.

AUNTIE LOO-LOO. *(darkly)* One never knows – these village girls. It's all very fine, *now* – but when the evenings start lengthening.

BRUCE. *(crossing to the window)* Those are the books from Mudie's.

CECILY. *(looking at one of the books)* What a ghastly picture! Really, Bruce, how you can read these horrible books! *(She shows the photograph to* AUNTIE LOO-LOO.*)*

AUNTIE LOO-LOO. *(reading)* "Actual photograph of the remains of – " Oo! How revolting! Before lunch, too. Are there anymore?

CECILY. What do you think of the house?

AUNTIE LOO-LOO. *(rising and meandering up centre to the staircase and round at back)* Oh, charming! Charming! Ideal – so quaint and picturesque – quite the little cottage o' dreams. Have you had it surveyed?

BRUCE. Oh, that's all right, Miss Garrard, I've had a pretty good look over it – I know something about these things.

AUNTIE LOO-LOO. Oh, yes, Canada! Well, it certainly has a most delightful atmosphere.

CECILY. That's just what I was saying.

AUNTIE LOO-LOO. You're sure there isn't any dry-rot?

CECILY. I haven't seen any.

AUNTIE LOO-LOO. You don't *see* dry-rot, my dear, it just goes on and on secretly for years and years until, finally, the whole place collapses on you.

BRUCE. It'll probably happen on my bath night?

AUNTIE LOO-LOO. So you have a bath?

BRUCE. Of course, and plenty of water.

AUNTIE LOO-LOO. *(crossing to* CECILY*)* Oh, I'm glad of that; it makes it seem a little less primitive. *(confidentially to* CECILY*)* I noticed at the bottom of the garden... so inconvenient on wet nights.

BRUCE. *(overhearing)* No, that's the tool-shed.

*(*CECILY *takes the books from the table up to the bookcase right centre.)*

AUNTIE LOO-LOO. *(embarrassed)* Oh – er – well, I mustn't stay here doing nothing, I must earn my lunch. Let me help with that trunk.

*(*BRUCE *and* AUNTIE LOO-LOO *go towards the trunk.* ETHEL *enters from the kitchen.)*

ETHEL. That china-cupboard's bung full, miss, what shall I do with the rest?

CECILY. I'll come and give you a hand.

AUNTIE LOO-LOO. Shall I – ?

CECILY. No, it's all right, Auntie Loo-Loo, Ethel and I can manage.

AUNTIE LOO-LOO. Yes, it does look a little small for three.

*(*CECILY *exits into the kitchen, followed by* ETHEL. AUNTIE LOO-LOO *watches her off.* BRUCE *has picked up a "Notable Trials" series book from the bookcase and is glancing at it in front of the fireplace.)*

Now then, what's the next thing to be done? *(She opens the japanned box and takes out an album.)* Snapshots!

*(*BRUCE *hurries across and snatches the book from her.)*

BRUCE. Excuse me, Miss Garrard!

AUNTIE LOO-LOO. Oh! Something I oughtn't to have seen?

BRUCE. No, not exactly that.

AUNTIE LOO-LOO. I believe it was. That pretty girl in the lovely shawl. Who is it?

BRUCE. That was my sister.

AUNTIE LOO-LOO. You needn't worry, my dear boy – I'm a woman of the world. Let me help you unpack it.

BRUCE. *(hastily closing the box and dragging it towards the cellar)* I can manage it myself. Thanks all the same. It's just my photography; I'll get it out of the way.

(He exits down into the cellar.)

AUNTIE LOO-LOO. You must look out for blackbeetles in that cellar.

(She wanders to the table behind the sofa and spots the shawl. CECILY enters.)

CECILY. Really, you know, I think Ethel's going to be quite good –

AUNTIE LOO-LOO. Where did you get this beautiful shawl, Cecily?

CECILY. Oh, yes, isn't it lovely – Bruce has just given it to me.

AUNTIE LOO-LOO. Oh, has he?

CECILY. We've had to put the rest of the china on the top shelf of the larder.

AUNTIE LOO-LOO. I hope you haven't bought a pig in a poke, dear. What did you pay for it?

CECILY. Fifteen hundred.

AUNTIE LOO-LOO. That seems a great deal to me.

(BRUCE re-enters from the cellar. CECILY goes to the trunk and continues unpacking books, photos, etcetera)

BRUCE. That cellar's going to make the best dark room I've ever had. There'll be a day's work down there clearing it up.

AUNTIE LOO-LOO. I've just been admiring the lovely shawl you've given Cecily.

BRUCE. *(picking up the gardening book from the table)* Is this your book, Miss Garrard?

AUNTIE LOO-LOO. Oh, yes, of course! Such a good book. I got it at the bookstall. Seven-and-six, reduced to a shilling. It's about gardening. We must have a look at it later.

CECILY. *(who is also undoing a parcel)* Oh, look! Here are my candlesticks. Here's the other one. *(She unwraps it and sees that it is broken.)* Oh!

AUNTIE LOO-LOO. *(having thought of a way out)* Those wretched moving men!

(HODGSON enters through the French window with a bunch of lilac centre)

HODGSON. The lilocks, mum.

CECILY. *(crossing to HODGSON and taking the lilac)* Thank you, Hodgson. How perfectly lovely. Look, Auntie Loo-Loo – out of the garden.

AUNTIE LOO-LOO. Just fancy! – Nothing to pay.

CECILY. *(calling into the kitchen)* Ethel, fill that jug with water, will you?

AUNTIE LOO-LOO. So this is your gardener, is it?

HODGSON. That's right, mum.

(ETHEL enters with a vase, hands it to CECILY and exits.)

AUNTIE LOO-LOO. *(crossing to HODGSON with the gardening book)* I think this book might be of use to him – *Every Day in My Garden.* There's a calendar which tells you what work to do every day in the year – now, let's see what it says for April.

HODGSON. *(starting to go)* I've managed this garden for thirty years without books, and I don't want to be...

(By the time she has got to "mulch" in her next speech he has ambled off into the garden.)

AUNTIE LOO-LOO. We must move with the times. Besides, this is different. *(searching in the book)* Now, what's today? Ah, yes, here we are. *(reading)* "Sow zinnias in pots – keep at a temperature of 60 degrees. Now is the time to mulch" – "mulch?" – what a funny word – "to mulch with newly rotted – er – manure – " *(She looks up.*) He's gone. I ought to have said fertilizer. *(making for the French window)* Wait a minute, gardener!

(She exits into the garden. **BRUCE** *and* **CECILY** *do their best to stifle their laughter.)*

BRUCE. Well, that was a nasty shock, wasn't it?

CECILY. I'm so sorry, dear, she meant it kindly.

BRUCE. Yes, of course, but – er – as long as she doesn't make a habit of it.

CECILY. I'll see she doesn't do that.

BRUCE. I resent anybody that stops me being alone with you – and when it's Auntie Loo-Loo –

CECILY. Don't say that or she'll come back. *(She goes to the window, looks out, and begins to laugh.)* It's all right, she's chasing Hodgson up and down the herbaceous border.

*(***BRUCE***, standing behind her, kisses the nape of her neck.)*

Perhaps he'll brain her with the spade.

*(***BRUCE*** moves away towards the cellar stairs.)*

You can see he's not listening to her even from this distance. She's cornered him now! *(She laughs again.)* You simply must come and watch this, she's…

(She looks at **BRUCE** *and sees that he has reeled and clutched at the post of the staircase. She runs to him.)*

Darling! What is it?

BRUCE. Nothing, nothing! I'm all right now.

CECILY. But what – what was it?

BRUCE. I just felt giddy for a moment, that's all. It's nothing! Perhaps it was seeing Auntie Loo-Loo suddenly like that.

CECILY. Come and sit down, darling.

(She leads him to the armchair.)

Sit down and rest. I think I'd better send for the doctor.

BRUCE. No, no, no, I don't want a doctor – I'm quite all right now.

CECILY. But, darling –

BRUCE. *(emphatically)* I don't want a doctor.

CECILY. *(starting to go to the kitchen)* I'll get you a glass of water.

BRUCE. No, no, don't bother.

CECILY. Is there anything I can get you? Is there anything you'd like?

BRUCE. Yes.

CECILY. What?

BRUCE. I'd like you to come and sit by me.

CECILY. *(doing so, on the left arm of the chair)* You're sure you're feeling better? *(She puts her arm round him.)*

BRUCE. *(with his head on her shoulder)* I'm perfectly all right now – as long as you don't go away.

CECILY. Of course I won't.

BRUCE. *(with his eyes closed)* Oh, this is heaven – at least it will be at three-fifteen.

CECILY. Why three-fifteen?

BRUCE. When Auntie Loo-Loo's train leaves.

(They laugh.)

CECILY. But, really, it is perfect, isn't it?

BRUCE. Very nearly.

CECILY. Only very nearly?

BRUCE. I mean that it's still growing. *(He merges into perfect English.)* It'll go on until it reaches absolute perfection – and then –

CECILY. And then?

BRUCE. And then – my darling – my precious – then you'll see how wonderful it will be.

CECILY. Darling – do you know you said that quite like an Englishman?

BRUCE. Did I?

(curtain)

Scene II

(Scene – The same. Early in September. It is a very fine afternoon.)

(As the curtain rises, **ETHEL** *is descending the two steps from the kitchen door with a tea-pot and hot-water jug. She puts them down on the table by the sofa and goes to the French windows.)*

ETHEL. *(yelling)* Tea! *(Then in a quiet afterthought.)* Mum... Mrs. Lovell... Te-ea!

(There is apparently no response. **ETHEL** *fetches rather a heavy brass bell from the ledge of the small window and rings it deafeningly at the garden.* **BRUCE** *appears, ascending from the cellar. His appearance and manner are slightly changed from the first time we saw him. He doesn't look nearly as well, he has lost a lot of that easy buoyancy, and now phases of abstraction, not at all melancholy, however, alternate with a tingle of suppressed elation. He carries a photographic dish with some snaps in it.* **ETHEL** *stops ringing and makes for the cellar stairs. She hasn't seen* **BRUCE**, *who is behind her, up stage centre)*

BRUCE. *(dangerously)* Where d'you think you're going?

ETHEL. Law, Mr. Lovell, you fair gave me a turn!

BRUCE. *(chuckling quietly)* Well, you can get it quite clear. I won't have you or anyone else muddling round in my dark room!

ETHEL. I'm sorry, sir. I was just coming down to tell you that tea's ready.

BRUCE. *(moving down centre)* I'd gathered that. *(In a more conciliatory manner.)* You are a clever girl to have learnt to cut such thin bread and butter; d'you remember those awful hunks you used to give us three months ago?

ETHEL. They don't care for it like that at 'ome.

BRUCE. I dare say not. Look, here's that snap I took last week of you and Don.

ETHEL. *(crossing to* BRUCE *and looking at the photo)* Oh, sir – that's fine!

BRUCE. Yes, I think it's rather good – of the dog.

ETHEL. *(taking him seriously)* Oh!

BRUCE. I'll let you have some to distribute amongst your many admirers.

ETHEL. Oh, Mr. Lovell!

(She exits into the kitchen. BRUCE *puts the dish on the table left centre and crosses to the mirror on the wall down stage left, where he examines the roots of his hair very closely. He suddenly hears* CECILY *calling to* HODGSON, *so hurries across and sits in the armchair by the tea-table, produces his notebook and starts looking through it.)*

*(*CECILY *comes in from the garden through the French windows, removing her gardening gloves. She throws a light silk scarf over the sofa arm, crosses to the table left centre and puts her gloves and hat on it, then returns to behind* BRUCE'*s chair.)*

CECILY. And what has our Mr. Pepys got in his diary for today?

BRUCE. *(laughing)* Wouldn't you like to know!

CECILY. What's H_2O_2 mean? It's the only thing you've got down for today. What is H_2O_2?

BRUCE. Only a chemical I'm going to use in my new developer.

CECILY. *(sitting centre of the sofa and starting to pour out tea)* Oh, your nasty old photography. Did you have a nice rest?

BRUCE. *(like a schoolboy who has been found out)* Well, I – er – that is to say, I –

CECILY. *Bruce!* I don't believe you had a rest at all!

(He shakes his head guiltily.)

Oh, Bruce! – you promised me! What did you do?

(CECILY, *during the following, eats a hearty tea.*)

BRUCE. *(pointing down towards the cellar)* I'm sorry, sweetheart, but I just felt restless.

CECILY. If only you'd see a doctor!

BRUCE. And have him popping in and out of the house every day of the week – not on your life!

CECILY. He need only come once – just a little advice.

BRUCE. Darling, don't let's go over all that again. I'm perfectly all right, honestly.

CECILY. You don't look all right, you haven't looked all right since that attack you had when we came here – and you're looking worse.

BRUCE. Aren't you a little ray of sunshine! It's been a very hot summer.

CECILY. Yes, but you've been used to all sorts of climates. If only we knew what it was.

BRUCE. Don't you worry, my dear, I know my own health. I'm as fit as a fiddle, it's just that my circulation gets a bit out of order sometimes, it's happened before.

CECILY. When? Have your tea, dear.

BRUCE. *(vaguely)* Oh, at – er – various intervals.

CECILY. You aren't worried about anything, are you?

BRUCE. Lord, no – do I seem worried?

CECILY. No... No, just a little bit absent-minded at moments.

BRUCE. *(smiling to himself)* Fancy!... I wasn't aware of it.

CECILY. It's only because I love you so that I fuss sometimes. I wonder if this place really agrees with you?

BRUCE. Well, if it doesn't, we shall be clearing out by the end of the month.

CECILY. It seems almost a pity, doesn't it?

BRUCE. What does?

CECILY. Leaving here when we've got things so nice.

BRUCE. But I thought you were always so anxious to travel?

CECILY. So I was – so I am – I'm fearfully excited – in a way, but it seems as though we've only just settled in.

BRUCE. Ah ha! Settled in! Where's that spirit of adventure we've heard so much about?

CECILY. It's still there all right, but I wish one could be in two places at once. Have you decided yet where we're to go first?

BRUCE. As a matter of fact I had an idea while you were in the garden.

CECILY. What is it?

BRUCE. How would it be if we had our passports viséd for everywhere?

CECILY. How d'you mean?

BRUCE. Well, then we needn't decide on anything till the very last moment. We'll just go to a ticket office and shut our eyes and stick a pin into a map.

CECILY. That's a wonderful idea, but –

BRUCE. It'll be quite easy, we shall be travelling light.

CECILY. You do think of the loveliest things.

BRUCE. Oh, I'm inspired by you, my angel. (*He takes her hand.*)

(*They draw apart at the click of the latch as* ETHEL *enters from the kitchen carrying letters in her hand. As she comes to* CECILY *she checks herself and goes offstage again.*)

What's the matter with her?

CECILY. Sh!

(ETHEL *returns with the letters on a tray.*)

ETHEL. The post, mum.

(*There is one for* CECILY *– three for* BRUCE.)

BRUCE. I always thought postmen delivered letters at the front door.

ETHEL. (*with infinite meaning*) Not this one doesn't, Mr. Lovell.

(She exits into the kitchen. **BRUCE** *opens a letter, then another, then one in a long envelope.)*

BRUCE. Oh, hum! *(He is lying.)* My solicitors say I shall be able to touch my capital soon. I hope to goodness it's before we go away. Who's your letter from?

CECILY. Mavis. She's just got back.

BRUCE. *(with a touch of coldness)* Oh. *(after a pause)* What does she say?

CECILY. She wants to be friends; she wants to make it up.

BRUCE. But you haven't quarrelled with her?

CECILY. Well, not really, but… well, you and she didn't hit it off very well, did you?

BRUCE. God knows, I did my best.

CECILY. Anyway, she wants to come down for the day.

BRUCE. When?

CECILY. Well, I don't know, but I should like her to see the garden before everything's over.

BRUCE. Do we really want people butting in?

CECILY. In any case, she can't come down often, can she?

BRUCE. Oh, yes, of course, I'd forgotten. *(With a change to a more affable manner.)* Yes… you'd want, in any case, to say good-bye. Well, supposing she comes down for the day on – let me see. *(He produces his notebook.)* Twentieth… twenty-first… ask her for the twenty-fifth, it's a Friday – that's a fortnight tomorrow, we shall be leaving on the Saturday. *(He makes a note.)* I say – she won't want to see us off, will she? I can't bear being "seen off."

CECILY. Neither can I.

BRUCE. We shall have to keep Auntie Loo-Loo at bay somehow.

CECILY. Oh, I don't think she'll attempt that – you squashed her pretty heavily last time she was here.

BRUCE. O.K., then ask Mavis for the twenty-fifth – but only for the day, mind.

CECILY. *(rising and moving down right)* Thank you, darling – it'll be nice to have the atmosphere a little friendlier. *(After a pause.)* She says something here about Nigel.

BRUCE. Oh, you're not going to ask *him?*

CECILY. Mavis seems to think that it's the idea that he can't see me that's upsetting him so much and that perhaps if we met again in a friendly spirit, he might be –

BRUCE. That's all baloney.

CECILY. Oh, well, all right… I believe you're jealous.

BRUCE. Maybe I am.

(CECILY *goes to him and puts her hand on his shoulder – he kisses it passionately. He raises his head suddenly, listening.*)

There's a car stopped at the end of the lane.

CECILY. *(nervously)* Oh… oh, yes, I'd forgotten.

BRUCE. *(amiably)* What?

(CECILY *backs a little. The following is played very quickly.*)

CECILY. Darling, promise me you won't be angry?

BRUCE. *(amiably)* What about?

CECILY. It's only because I was so anxious.

BRUCE. *(pleasantly impatient)* Come on, honey, spill it.

CECILY. I sent a message this morning when you were out.

BRUCE. A message?

CECILY. To Dr. Gribble.

BRUCE. *(in sudden fury – rising)* Damn it! Why did you do that?

CECILY. Bruce, darling, please!

BRUCE. I've told you again and again I hate and detest doctors… lot of blasted quacks.

CECILY. I couldn't help it, Bruce, I was so anxious.

BRUCE. I won't have people interfering and fussing round here.

CECILY. He's very well thought of in the village.

BRUCE. *(turning furiously away to the windows)* What do *they* know? – pack of half-baked yokels.

CECILY. You will see him, dear?… just to please me?

BRUCE. Well, I don't see how I can very well turn him out of the house.

(There is a knock on the front door.)

CECILY. Here he is. *(She goes to the door and opens it.)*

DR. GRIBBLE. *(offstage)* Ah – Mrs. Lovell?

CECILY. Yes – good afternoon, doctor.

*(**DR. GRIBBLE** enters. He is about sixty – a man of intense charm and sweetness of manner. Even **BRUCE**, with his antipathy to doctors, succumbs at once.)*

DR. GRIBBLE. *(coming down)* Well, well, you *are* hidden away here, aren't you?

CECILY. *(left of* **DR. GRIBBLE***)* This is my husband, Dr. Gribble.

DR. GRIBBLE. *(crossing down below the tea-table)* How do you do?… Yes, I've only been up this lane two or three times in my life.

BRUCE. We're fairly remote… and peaceful.

DR. GRIBBLE. Ah, peace – that's a rare luxury nowadays… I see you've got old Hodgson working for you in the garden.

BRUCE. He's a funny old chap.

CECILY. I think he's a dear.

DR. GRIBBLE. He's a real old scoundrel, isn't he… when he's had a drop too much he calls me "Old Doctor Kill-or-Cure," at the top of his voice outside the Red Lion.

*(They laugh, except **BRUCE**. **CECILY** speaks the next line to cover an awkward pause.)*

CECILY. Won't you have some tea?

DR. GRIBBLE. No, thank you; I've had my tea. Well, now, your wife wants me to have a look at you, I understand?

BRUCE. It's really nothing at all. You know what women are.

DR. GRIBBLE. No harm in having an overhaul now and then. Where can we – ?

CECILY. Perhaps upstairs.

DR. GRIBBLE. *(starting for the stairs)* Thank you. *(He turns and sees that* BRUCE *hasn't moved, so speaks to him.)* Will you lead the way?

BRUCE. O.K. *(He goes upstairs.)* But I'm sure we're bothering you for nothing.

DR. GRIBBLE, *(as he follows him)* Never mind, I always say it would be a very good thing if people wouldn't wait until they were really ill before calling in the doctor.

(They both disappear.)

CECILY. *(crossing to the kitchen door and calling)* Ethel! Clear the tea things, will you?

(ETHEL enters and fetches the tray.)

Oh, by the way, Ethel. Where's my old scarf? I had to use that one this afternoon.

ETHEL. I thought you knew, mum.

CECILY. Knew what?

ETHEL. I found it yesterday torn to bits –

CECILY. Oh!

ETHEL. It's that wretched dog, mum. 'E's bin at it again.

CECILY. Yes, it really is wicked of him.

ETHEL. Yes, isn't it? You try to scold him – but you know the way he looks at you, you haven't got the heart.

CECILY. Never mind; it's only an old scarf.

ETHEL. Oh, I thought it was ever so pretty.

CECILY. Did you?

ETHEL. Yes. Me sister Nellie's got one ever so –

(HODGSON has appeared in the French windows.)

CECILY. Hullo, Hodgson; what have you got there?

(ETHEL exits to the kitchen.)

HODGSON. *(entering with a small earth-stained sack)* I was wondering if you knew anything about this, mum?

CECILY. What is it?

HODGSON. I don't know; that's what I was coming up to ask you. Digged it up I did – over by that south wall.

CECILY. Perhaps it's hidden treasure – how exciting. Bring it in and let's have a look.

(**HODGSON** *brings the sack over to the table.*)

Here's a paper. It isn't wet, is it? *(She spreads the paper on the table.)*

HODGSON. Not with this dry summer it isn't, mum, and I reckon it 'asn't been there long, earth was middlin' loose around it.

CECILY. Shall I fetch a knife?

HODGSON. *(right of the table)* I can manage with me fingers, mum, can't abide cutting string. There! *(He opens the sack and produces a smallish bottle.)* A bottle.

CECILY. *(upstage left corner of table)* A bottle of what?

HODGSON. Well, it was a bottle of – what's this yere on the label. PER – PER –

CECILY. Hydrogen peroxide. What else is there?

HODGSON. *(producing several more bottles)* Don't seem much like 'idden treasure to me, mum.

CECILY. No.

HODGSON. Lot of empty bottles!

CECILY. Well, there's nothing very mysterious about that, Hodgson.

HODGSON. But I don't see 'ow they could have got there without me knowing it unless they were digged in the night. You don't know anything about them?

CECILY. No, I certainly don't.

HODGSON. Maybe, Mr. Lovell –

CECILY. They may be something to do with his photography.

HODGSON. Aw, photography! Shall I put them on the rubbish heap!

CECILY. No, leave them. I'll ask Mr. Lovell when he comes down – he's upstairs with the doctor at present.

HODGSON. Aye, I saw doctor arriving. Nothing serious with the master I 'ope, mum?

CECILY. No, no, I don't think so, but I've been a little anxious about him lately.

HODGSON. A change of air'll do him good – more good than any doctor – Ethel tells me you're goin' to foreign parts, mum.

CECILY. Yes, at the end of the month.

HODGSON. That'll make him all right.

(He starts to exit to the garden. CECILY *puts the newspaper, sack and bottles under the table, and has just finished when* DR. GRIBBLE *comes down the stairs.)*

DR. GRIBBLE. Hullo, Hodgson. How's the rheumatics?

HODGSON. Oh, they've gone.

DR. GRIBBLE. I told you they would.

HODGSON. In God's good time.

(He exits into the garden through the French windows.)

CECILY. Well, doctor?

DR. GRIBBLE. *(coming down centre)* He'll be down in a minute, he's just putting his things on.

CECILY. But the examination – ?

DR. GRIBBLE. *(not as happy as he would have* CECILY *believe)* Oh, that's all right, Mrs. Lovell, nothing much wrong with him.

CECILY. Oh, I'm so glad.

DR. GRIBBLE. Just one thing, Mrs. Lovell – your husband isn't worried about anything?… Er – business matters?

CECILY. No.

DR. GRIBBLE. Or, possibly some little domestic anxiety?

CECILY. No, oh, no. I'm sure he'd have told me if he had any business worries.

DR. GRIBBLE. I asked him myself, of course, but he said "no" most emphatically, but I thought perhaps you might know of –

CECILY. No, no, nothing at all – why do you ask?

DR. GRIBBLE. Well, as a matter of fact – mark you, it isn't at all serious – but I think your husband is suffering from some slight myo-cardial condition.

CECILY. What is that? Heart?

DR. GRIBBLE. Yes. It's nothing to be alarmed about, but he mustn't over-exert himself; his pulse is one hundred and twenty.

CECILY. That's very high, isn't it?

DR. GRIBBLE. No, but we don't want it to get any worse. He's rather an excitable type of man, isn't he?

CECILY. Oh, no, I shouldn't say that – perhaps he's been a little bit nervy lately.

DR. GRIBBLE. Well, he became quite agitated when I suggested he might see a specialist – he absolutely refused.

CECILY. Do you think he'll be well enough to travel? We're intending to go abroad at the end of the month.

DR. GRIBBLE. Oh, yes, I think so – yes, certainly, as long as he takes things quietly in the meantime. I'll send along some medicine.

(Looking round, then wandering up to the bookcase.) You've made things very snug here, Mrs. Lovell.)

CECILY. Thank you.

DR. GRIBBLE. *(looking at the books)* All the *Notable Trials* series – I see you're interested in criminology.

CECILY. Oh, no, it's my husband, he's very keen.

DR. GRIBBLE. *(interested)* Really? So am I.

CECILY. Personally I find it rather a morbid study.

DR. GRIBBLE. Oh, no, surely not, if you approach it in the right spirit.

CECILY. Scientific, you mean? I'm afraid I can't keep it up, I always get the horrors.

DR. GRIBBLE. Ah, a pity!... I have quite a nice little library of criminology myself, it would be interesting to have some chats with your husband, he might like to borrow some of my books.

CECILY. That's very kind of you.

DR. GRIBBLE. Well, I must be getting along. I'm late for my surgery – I'll look in again in a day or so.

CECILY. *(dubiously)* You think it's necessary...?

DR. GRIBBLE. Ah, I know. You're thinking of your husband's objection to us poor medicos – yes, he told me, but I flatter myself that I managed to overcome them – we got on capitally – well, good-bye.

CECILY. Good-bye, doctor, and thank you so much.

DR. GRIBBLE. *(in the doorway up right)* That's a remarkably fine second crop of antirrhinum.

CECILY. Ah, but you should have seen the first.

DR. GRIBBLE. *(in the distance)* My dahlias look like being rather fine this year – you must come and see them, if you don't go away.

CECILY. *(in the doorway)* I should love to if we don't –

*(She breaks off, considering the possibility of the **DOCTOR**'s last remark being significant. **BRUCE** enters down the staircase, fastening his jacket and setting his tie.)*

BRUCE. Nice old codger that!

CECILY. I'm glad you liked him.

BRUCE. *(sincerely)* Yes, I did... *(He checks himself.)* He mustn't become a habit.

CECILY. No, of course not – let's hope there'll be no need.

BRUCE. He hasn't been scaring you about me, I hope?

CECILY. No, rather not – he says you've got to go quietly for a bit, that's all.

BRUCE. Well, I'll be good, I promise you.

CECILY. *(going to him)* Darling!

(They embrace, standing upstage centre)

Look what Hodgson dug up in the garden. *(She gets the bottles from under the table.)*

BRUCE. What? *(He moves casually to see and stops dead.)*

CECILY. *(who is intent on the bottles)* A lot of old peroxide bottles. Hodgson says they can't have been there very long. *(pause)* Isn't it a funny thing? *(She looks up at him.)*

BRUCE. *(quietly)* Yes, very odd.

CECILY. There's some left in this one.

BRUCE. Is there? Very wasteful. *(He puts the bottle down on the table.)*

CECILY. Do you know anything about them?

BRUCE. No – of course not.

CECILY. Oh, well, another of life's great unsolved mysteries. I'll put them on the rubbish heap. Hodgson and I hoped it was buried treasure! *(She collects the bottles except for the one which **BRUCE** has set aside.)* And then I must finish off my job before the light goes – Hodgson has been showing me how to make rose cuttings.

BRUCE. I'll come and help you.

CECILY. No, darling – don't forget what Dr. Gribble said. You sit and read – you promised to be good, remember. *(She picks up her gardening gloves.)*

BRUCE. Oh, very well. Don't be too long.

*(**CECILY** exits into the garden through the French windows.)*

*(Left alone **BRUCE** comes slowly and picks up the scarf on the arm of the sofa. He is smiling pleasantly to himself. He bends his head over the scarf sentimentally and rubs his face against it gently, then slowly he raises his head, and you can see that his expression has changed to an extent that is utterly terrifying. He stands very still – he is trembling violently and increasingly. As he begins to tear the scarf to pieces –)*

(The curtain falls)

ACT THREE

Scene I

(Scene – The same. It is late afternoon about a fortnight after – the light is very golden on the empty stage. (See Property Plot.))

(MAVIS and CECILY are heard off through the front door.)

CECILY. *(off)* Down, Don, *down!*

(Barking is heard.)

He always behaves like this in front of visitors – oh, you bad dog! No – Don, I won't have you in.

MAVIS. *(entering)* Do let him in.

CECILY. No, he's a darling, but so destructive. I've found scarves and gloves of mine torn to pieces recently.

MAVIS. *(sitting on the sofa)* Oh, that's different.

CECILY. No – no, you stay there, Don. *(She shuts the door and moves down right, putting the dog's lead on the sofa table as she passes.)* Oh, damn!

MAVIS. What's the matter?

CECILY. *(at the French windows)* I've forgotten to pick those flowers for you.

MAVIS. Never mind.

CECILY. Oh, no, no, I can't let you go back without some flowers. I'll ask Hodgson. *(she calls out:)* Hodgson!

HODGSON. *(in the distance)* Yes, mum?

CECILY. Pick a large bunch of flowers, will you, and tie them up, they're for Miss Wilson to take back to London.

HODGSON. *(off)* Very good, mum.

CECILY. *(to* MAVIS, *as she crosses up left)* What a ridiculous place this is, having no decent train after eight o'clock. *(She takes off her coat and leaves it on the banisters.)*

MAVIS. *(looking at the grandfather clock)* What's the time now?

CECILY. It's no good looking at that clock, we've lost the key. It hasn't been going for weeks. *(She goes to the cupboard by the stairs.)* It can't be much after seven – have a drink.

MAVIS. Yes, I could do with a whisky and soda after that walk. It was grand, though.

(CECILY pours out drinks at the cupboard.)

CECILY. Bruce will probably be down before you go, to say good-bye.

MAVIS. Somehow I rather doubt that.

CECILY. Oh, but you seemed to be getting on much better this time.

MAVIS. It was only by us both exercising the greatest control, and he was at the end of his tether by the time he'd finished tea. He did the wisest thing in going up to lie down.

CECILY. *(crossing to the sofa with drink)* But he lies down every afternoon – he really isn't well, you know. *(She returns to the cupboard for her own drink.)*

MAVIS. That's obvious. I've never seen such a change in a man.

CECILY. And he's not improving, quite the reverse in fact, in spite of having followed the doctor's advice and keeping quiet. *(She pulls the chair from above the table across to up left of the sofa.)*

MAVIS. Well, now that we're on the subject, I do think – you won't mind me saying it? –

CECILY. Of course not.

MAVIS. – but I do think it's extremely unwise of you to set off on your travels tomorrow with Bruce in that condition.

CECILY. *(sitting in the chair she has brought)* My dear, I know, but he's determined.

MAVIS. Can't you make him see sense?

CECILY. I've done everything I can. We had a – we almost had a scene about it before you arrived this morning.

MAVIS. How about the doctor?

CECILY. I'm afraid that's no use. He was very nearly rude to Dr. Gribble when he called yesterday.

MAVIS. Well, I do hope you'll be all right – of course, it's useless for me to attempt to – hullo!

(She picks up BRUCE's *notebook which is on the sofa.)*

Is this yours?

CECILY. *(stretching and taking the notebook)* No, it's Bruce's notebook. It's not like him to leave things about, he's so frightfully tidy – and methodical. He makes notes and memorandums of the quaintest things... I wonder what he's got down for today?

MAVIS. Doesn't he mind you reading his secrets?

CECILY. Not a bit; he's often shown it to me. Ah, here we are, September twenty-fifth – "Mavis for the day."

MAVIS. Dear me, I'm honoured.

CECILY. Told you so. Then there's another note. "Nine P.M."

MAVIS. H'm. Nine P.M. What's that – an assignation?

CECILY. Darling, he would be very clever if he started anything like that here. Believe it or not, but Ethel is the village beauty. No, I think it's to remind him about clearing up the dark room.

MAVIS. *(almost to herself)* What a very trivial thing to make a note about.

CECILY. Really, this notebook is too funny. Listen to this. *(reading)* "March twenty-fifth, marry Cecily. April seventh, get your hair cut" – that comes in regularly once a fortnight. "April fifteenth. Move into the cottage." *(to herself)* Silly... then there's this chemical stuff H_2O_2. It comes in regularly every week since the beginning of the year.

MAVIS. H_2O_2?

CECILY. It's something he uses for his photography.

MAVIS. *Does* one use peroxide in photography?

CECILY. H_2O_2 isn't peroxide.

MAVIS. Surely it is. Yes, H_2O_2 *is* hydrogen peroxide.

CECILY. How do you know?

MAVIS. I clean my teeth with it sometimes, the formula is often on the label.

CECILY. That's funny. I didn't notice it.

MAVIS. Notice what?

CECILY. Well, Hodgson dug up a whole lot of empty peroxide bottles and when I asked Bruce, he said he knew nothing about it... and yet here's peroxide occurring regularly in his notebook.

MAVIS. Perhaps his hair is going a bit grey and he's touching it up.

CECILY. Oh, don't be silly.

MAVIS. I dare say there are some "silver threads amongst the gold" and he's keeping it secret. *(She takes her cigarette-case from her handbag.)*

CECILY. Nonsense! *(putting the notebook down on the sofa table and rising)* Oh, don't smoke those – I've got some.

(She goes to the table left centre for the cigarette-box. MAVIS *takes a cigarette.)*

MAVIS. You're still using that dear old *Arabian Nights* cigarette-box.

CECILY. *(returning to the table with the cigarette-box)* Of course. I couldn't part with that... Nigel gave it to me.

MAVIS. I hadn't forgotten. *(She gets matches from her bag and lights her cigarette.)*

CECILY. *(returning to the chair and sitting)* You said that as though you thought I had... you're wrong, I often think of Nigel.

MAVIS. Listen, Cecily, won't you see him?

CECILY. Would it really be any help to him?

MAVIS. He wants nothing more than your friendship. He can't bear to think that all the years you were engaged, all the understanding, has come to nothing at all.

CECILY. It does seem a terrible pity. But it's no use now – not for heaven knows how long, we're going away tomorrow.

MAVIS. My dear, I've got a confession to make...

CECILY. Well? What is it?

MAVIS. I didn't come down by train – it wasn't the station taxi that dropped me at the top of the lane – it was Nigel's car.

CECILY. What?

MAVIS. He's here now.

CECILY. Where?

MAVIS. In the village waiting at the pub – The Blue Pig or whatever it is.

CECILY. The Red Lion.

MAVIS. We've had a "little conspiracy," as Auntie Loo-Loo would say.

CECILY. What about?

MAVIS. I arranged for him to meet me here at half-past seven. If the atmosphere was at all difficult I was to stop him at the top of the lane.

CECILY. But d'you think –

MAVIS. *(rising)* Oh, Nigel won't stay more than five minutes, and if Bruce comes down I'll square things with him.

CECILY. It would be lovely to see him again, but really I don't know that I –

(HODGSON enters through the French windows with a large bunch of flowers.)

MAVIS. Oh, aren't they lovely!

(CECILY rises and puts the chair back at the table.)

HODGSON. It hasn't left much show in the herbaceous border, mum, but that won't matter you goin' away tomorrow.

CECILY. Hodgson is very proud of his border, aren't you?

MAVIS. I'm not surprised – the whole garden looks perfectly lovely. What are these?

HODGSON. Penstemons, mum.

MAVIS. Penstem – oh, perhaps you're right.

HODGSON. Oh, it's a proper enough place if you don't mind being lonely.

MAVIS. *(upstage centre)* It certainly is a bit off the map.

HODGSON. Yes, miss, that's why Mr. Dunning let the place go so cheap.

CECILY. *(behind the table left centre)* Oh, I don't know that I should call fifteen hundred pounds cheap exactly.

MAVIS. Is that what you paid?

HODGSON. Fifteen 'undred pounds! Never, mum! *(He puts the flowers on the chair right of the fireplace.)* Nine hundred and fifty pounds Mr. Dunning was askin' for it, beggin' yer pardon – nine hundred and fifty pounds.

CECILY. Oh, no, Hodgson, you're wrong.

HODGSON. You'll excuse me, mum, but it were common talk in the village – why, I even 'eard Mr. Dunning 'imself saying that was the most 'e could ask for it, complained about it, 'e did; sayin' that 'e'd be out of pocket with all the money 'e'd spent on the place an' all.

(During HODGSON's speech CECILY has gone to the sofa table for the empty glasses. She now returns and puts them on the table left centre)

CECILY. Well, I don't care what Mr. Dunning said, we never met him, my husband did it all through the agents, but I do know the price because I wrote the cheque myself.

HODGSON. Well, I dare say you knows best, mum but nine 'undred and fifty pounds was the price we understood in the village. Fifteen 'undred pounds! That wouldn't be including the twenty-acre meadow?

CECILY. No, no, just for the house.

HODGSON. Well, would it be – ?

MAVIS. (*coming down centre to* HODGSON *and interrupting him*) The flowers are lovely!

HODGSON. Well, I'd better finish disbudding them chrysthanthemums before I go 'ome.

(*He exits through the French window.*)

MAVIS. (*at lower end of sofa*) What a funny thing!

CECILY. Oh, my dear, the most marvellous stories go round this village – I once had a cherry-brandy at the Red Lion and they've said I'm a dipsomaniac ever since – not that we know anybody, but I get all the scandal from Ethel.

MAVIS. But you bought the house yourself?

CECILY. No, no, I just advanced the money because Bruce's was tied up for the moment – you know – securities, solicitors and all that.

MAVIS. Oh I see.

(*The dog barks.* MAVIS *looks out of the window.*)

It's Nigel!

(*There is a knock on the door.* CECILY *goes to the door and opens it and reveals* NIGEL *on the doorstep. They stand looking at each other for quite a long time.*)

CECILY. (*quietly*) You are looking well.

NIGEL. (*smiling*) May I come in? (*He moves down centre.*)

CECILY. Please.

MAVIS. I'm going to watch Hodgson disbudding chrys*th*anthemums – whatever that may be – I hope it's nothing rude!

(*She exits into the garden.*)

CECILY. Mavis has gone all "Auntie Loo-Loo."

NIGEL. It *is* good to see you.

CECILY. It's not so bad seeing you again. *(She moves towards him impulsively.)* Oh, you don't know how I've wanted to tell you... Have a cigarette! Have a drink! –

NIGEL. Half a moment, let's take this quite calmly. Come on, let's sit down.

(They sit side by side on the sofa.)

CECILY. *(after a pause)* Well?

NIGEL. Well?

(They both laugh.)

CECILY. I'm longing to hear all your news. You've no idea how glad I am to see you looking so fit.

NIGEL. That was one of the reasons I wanted to see you. I didn't want you to go away on your travels with the idea that you'd turned me into a shuddering drug-fiend or anything like that.

CECILY. *(laughing)* Oh, don't!

NIGEL. And you? You're happy?

CECILY. Enormously.

NIGEL. I'm glad.

CECILY. That's sweet of you.

NIGEL. No, honestly I am. I'm not being all noble – "Eric or Little by Little." Just because I can't have you myself it doesn't mean I've become bitter and resent your marriage being a success.

CECILY. It is – a grand success. Of course, I suppose one can't expect...

NIGEL. What?

CECILY. Well, I mean Bruce's health has been a bit of a worry since we've been here, but the change will put him right I'm sure.

NIGEL. Where are you going?

CECILY. Anywhere – everywhere!

NIGEL. Ah, that's what you've always wanted.

CECILY. Yes, but you know it's a funny thing, now it comes to the point I'm awfully sorry to be leaving here.

(NIGEL *laughs.*)

Yes, I know. I'm a perverse idiot, aren't I?

NIGEL. So was I when you turned me down. I was very stupid and pig-headed with you. That old Sudan had made me stodgy –

CECILY. Oh, no!

NIGEL. Oh, yes, it had – too much tinned asparagus and sand in your ears!

(*They both laugh.*)

CECILY. I can't have you taking any blame.

NIGEL. No. You had been unsettled by your money – my imagination had gone dull, and I didn't really understand – and that's that.

CECILY. I think it's grand of you to be so generous about it.

NIGEL. Don't you run away with the idea that I don't still care for you – I do. And don't say, "You'll meet some nice girl one day" – I shan't!

CECILY. Right. When do you start work in your London office?

NIGEL. Said she, tactfully changing the subject. In a month's time. The Wentworths have asked me up to Scotland till then for some shooting.

CECILY. How very social.

NIGEL. Social! – suicidal if you get anywhere near Stanley Wentworth.

CECILY. I suppose there'll be awful photographs in *The Tatler.*

NIGEL. I expect so.

CECILY. Do you suppose Alice Wentworth can get all that on a shooting-stick?

(*They both roll with laughter.*)

NIGEL. She might manage with two. I'm motoring up tomorrow – I want to do it in the day if I can. I shall have to start at the crack of dawn. Why "crack"

– extraordinary expressions we have in the English language.

(**MAVIS** *enters through the French windows.* **NIGEL** *rises.*)

MAVIS. Well, I've learned all about disbudding chrys*th*anthemums – I should hate to have it done to me. (*Looking towards the stairs.*) Well, I don't know; I don't want to break up the party, but I think perhaps we ought to be getting back. Got to get up early tomorrow, you know, Nigel.

CECILY. (*rising and moving down centre, then to the kitchen door*) Oh, no, no, it's so lovely having you both here. You must have something to eat before you go anyway.

MAVIS. (*following her, then stopping centre*) How about – er? (*She glances upstairs.*)

CECILY. Oh, yes – well – I – wait a moment, I'll pop up and see him.

(*She runs upstairs.*)

NIGEL. I say, Mavis, old girl, I'm frightfully grateful to you for –

MAVIS. My dear Nigel, you know exactly how I feel about the whole business. Do you feel better about things now?

NIGEL. Yes…

MAVIS. (*sitting on the chair above the table*) Good.

NIGEL. … She does seem to be really happy, doesn't she?

MAVIS. Do you think so?

NIGEL. (*centre*) I'm asking you.

MAVIS. As a matter of fact, Nigel, there are one or two things – quite apart from the fact that I don't like the man – there are one or two things that strike me as distinctly odd.

NIGEL. How d'you mean?

MAVIS. Well, his appearance has altered so much – he looks almost alarming.

NIGEL. Alarming?

MAVIS. I'm sure there's something serious the matter with him. I think it absolutely fantastic Cecily going abroad with him tomorrow.

NIGEL. Isn't he seeing a doctor or something?

MAVIS. Yes, but he doesn't seem to have any influence with him. I wish we could get the low-down from the doctor himself. Another thing – there seems to be some queer muddle over the price of the house.

NIGEL. The price of the house?

MAVIS. The whole thing strikes me as extremely fishy – then I've just discovered that Bruce –

(At this moment they hear BRUCE's voice from the room upstairs – only because it is obviously raised.)

BRUCE. (offstage, faintly) That's too much! That woman's been here all day and now that man – no! I won't have it – you can cut the idea right out!

(MAVIS and NIGEL look at each other. There is a pause.)

MAVIS. (rising) We shall have to get along, Nigel.

NIGEL. Obviously. I don't quite like – What was that you were saying about the house?

MAVIS. Well, you see, Bruce – ssh! – she's coming.

NIGEL. Let's have dinner somewhere. That pub in the village?

MAVIS. Yes, we'll go to the Pig and Whistle. I'll tell you there.

NIGEL. (moving up to the fireplace) Yes – and we might go and rout out that doctor afterwards.

MAVIS. (moving down in front of the sofa) Yes. He'll probably curse us for calling so late, but I think we ought to.

(CECILY comes downstairs with a slightly despondent droop.)

CECILY. (standing at the foot of the stairs) I'm so sorry, Bruce is feeling rather off-colour – a bit nervy. He's had a long day – you see, and –

NIGEL. Oh, that's all right; we quite understand. After all's said and done, it is a bit awkward.

MAVIS. We shan't be back in Town till very late as it is.

CECILY. *(crossing down to* **MAVIS***)* Oh, I do so wish you hadn't to go. It's been so lovely seeing you both *(she turns towards* **NIGEL***, who has come down centre)* – all three of us here in the country… It's like that time when we were at that place – oh, you know – what is it? – that place where the river's very wide and there is a weir. *(She moves to* **MAVIS** *and flings her arms round her.)* Good-bye, darling, it's been heaven today. *(She goes to* **NIGEL***, hesitates a moment, and then flings her arms round him.)* Good-bye, I shall see you when we come home. Have a lovely time in Scotland.

MAVIS. You'll write to us, won't you, my dear?

CECILY. Of course I shall – if we're not out of touch with a Post Office.

NIGEL. Ah ha! "Mrs. Livingstone I presume!" You'll be back when, do you think?

CECILY. Next spring, or early summer, I expect.

NIGEL. Come on, Mavis.

(They are at the front door now.)

CECILY. Good-bye, my dears.

MAVIS. You're sure you're all right?

CECILY. Yes, of course.

MAVIS. Well, I'll tell you what I'll do – I'll ring you up when we get back, to say good night.

CECILY. A charming thought, dear, but we're not on the 'phone.

MAVIS. Not on the 'phone! What do you use – carrier pigeons?

(She goes.)

NIGEL. Good-bye. *(He pauses.)* Er – well – take care of yourself.

(*He exits.* CECILY *shuts the door and moves down right centre.* HODGSON *enters through the French windows carrying a rose behind his back.*)

CECILY. (*left of the sofa*) Ah, Hodgson, finished with the chrys*th*anthemums?

HODGSON. Yes, mum, I be off 'ome now as I've got to make an early start tomorrow. Thought I'd look in and wish you good-bye.

CECILY. That's very kind of you, Hodgson.

(ETHEL *enters from the kitchen with her hat and coat on.*)

Ethel – the flowers – run after them.

(ETHEL *hurtles off through the front door with the flowers.*)

HODGSON. I'll keep a good eye on things while you're away – you can rely on me.

CECILY. I'm sure I can.

HODGSON. That is, as soon as I get back – if I'm able to move when they've finished with me at that there hospital.

CECILY. Well, we must get rid of those rheumatics for you before the winter – and they can't do much harm to you in a day.

HODGSON. Perhaps you're right, mum, but I'm only going because the master's sending me, and you can't look a gift horse in the mouth.

CECILY. Take things easy – don't work too hard.

HODGSON. It's a pleasure working for anyone as fond of flowers as you are, mum – and I was thinking you might like a buttonhole for your dress this evening. (*He produces the rose from behind his back.*) It's the last one left on the prize standard in the corner.

CECILY. (*taking it*) Oh, it's divine – "The Last Rose of Summer." (*She moves to the table left centre*)

(HODGSON *roars with laughter.*)

HODGSON. Vicar's wife sang that song at the concert at Christmas – "The Last Rose of Summer" – it sent me out for the last drink of the evening. *(more laughter)*

(**ETHEL** *re-enters, puffing excitedly, moves down and stands centre.*)

ETHEL. Oo! The gentleman gave me ten shillin'.

CECILY. That was very kind of him.

ETHEL. That makes a 'ole pound with the ten shillin' the master gave me.

HODGSON. See you save that up, my girl.

CECILY. The *master* gave you?

ETHEL. Yes, on top of me wages – ten shillin' he give me to go to the fair tonight.

CECILY. I'd no idea there *was* any fair.

ETHEL. Yes'm, it always comes late in the year 'ereabouts and master said I could go 'ome early, and it didn't matter how late I stayed at the fair as I wouldn't be wanted in the morning.

CECILY. Well, this is the first I've heard of all this.

ETHEL. *(crestfallen)* Oh, then – please, mum, shan't I – ?

HODGSON. Of course you won't; you'll stay as long as you're wanted.

CECILY. *(smiling)* That's all right, Ethel, the master's right, there's no real need – yes, you can go.

ETHEL. Oh, thank you, mum – thank you. *(She goes to the door left)*

HODGSON. You're spoiling her, mum.

CECILY. Oh, am I? Well, I'll spoil you too, you may as well finish this whisky. You go with Ethel, she'll give you a glass in the kitchen.

HODGSON. No need for a glass. Thank you kindly, mum.

CECILY. I shan't be seeing you again, Ethel.

ETHEL. Oh, Lor', mum, that fair had put it clean out of my head. Well, good-bye, mum, I hope you have a nice time.

CECILY. Thank you, Ethel. You'll look after things, won't you, while I'm away?

ETHEL. That I will, mum – an' I'll have a rare old spring-cleanin' for when you comes back.

CECILY. We'll give you good warning about that.

ETHEL. Everythin's ready for supper, I think, mum. I've put all the things on the tray. Will there be anythin' else, mum?

CECILY. No, thank you, Ethel. *(She points to the glasses on the table.)* Take these glasses, will you?

(ETHEL picks them up.)

Enjoy yourself at the fair – who are you going with? That nice postman?

ETHEL. *(contemptuously)* Oh, him! No, m'm, I'm goin' with Ted Saunders, who brings the milk.

(She exits into the kitchen.)

CECILY. Oh, I see. Well, good-bye, Hodgson. Oh, here's Don's lead. *(She takes it from the sofa table and gives it to him.)* I'd forgotten. Take good care of him, won't you?

HODGSON. Don't you worry, mum. I'll look after him.

CECILY. Good-bye, Hodgson. Take care of that rheumatism.

HODGSON. I will. Good-bye – good luck, mum.

(He exits after ETHEL into the kitchen. CECILY puts the rose down on the sofa table and makes for the staircase. DR. GRIBBLE enters through the front door. As CECILY gets to the second stair he speaks.)

DR. GRIBBLE. May I come in?

CECILY. *(with a touch of dismay)* Oh, good evening, Dr. Gribble; I wasn't expecting you.

DR. GRIBBLE. This isn't exactly a professional visit, Mrs. Lovell. I'm very anxious not to disturb your husband more than is necessary, but I do really feel that it's most unwise for him to go away at present.

CECILY. *(moving downstage)* Why? Do you think he's worse?

DR. GRIBBLE. *(standing in front of the sofa)* Well, I'm not at all happy about him. Where is he now?

CECILY. He's upstairs, resting.

DR. GRIBBLE. Don't disturb him.

CECILY. He'll be down soon for supper.

DR. GRIBBLE. I want you to let me make one more effort to get him to see reason.

CECILY. If only you could – but –

DR. GRIBBLE. It occurred to me –

CECILY. Do sit down.

DR. GRIBBLE. Oh, thank you very much. *(He puts his hat, slick and a book he has been carrying on the sofa and sits at upstage end of it.)* It occurred to me that if I were to have a chat with him on some other subject, I might be able to win his confidence a little more. So I've brought him the latest of the *Notable Trials* series. I've just finished reading it. *The Trial of "Frankie" Bellingham,* the papers were full of it last year – it was extremely interesting – American case.

CECILY. Yes, I seem to remember something –

DR. GRIBBLE. Well, he was tried for attempted murder, but he was brilliantly defended and he got an acquittal. Of course, it was in America. Later evidence came to hand that showed that he was guilty beyond all possible doubt. But he'd disappeared by then. *(turning over the pages of the book)* And yet he was quite a pleasant-looking fellow. There he is, look, Mrs. Lovell.

(He shows her the photograph. She looks at it over the upstage arm of the sofa.)

Really quite nice looking. You can see why they nicknamed him "Frankie."

CECILY. I don't like the moustache or the eyeglass or the buttonhole.

DR. GRIBBLE. Oh, that was part of the pose he adopted – the American idea of the typical Englishman – they said in the States that he was an Oxford man, but I don't think that's likely.

CECILY. No?

DR. GRIBBLE. Murdering five women seems rather too rough for Oxford. These mass murderers are nearly all the same – it would seem that they get worked up to a certain pitch of insanity and then the crime itself apparently clears their brains for a while. Anyhow, it's fascinating reading. I'm sure it'll interest your husband, knowing America as he does.

CECILY. *(taking the book from him)* Oh, but how silly I am. I'm almost certain Bruce has got the book already.

DR. GRIBBLE. Oh, how very disappointing.

CECILY. *(moving up to the bookcase)* He's been reading it recently. Now where is it? Ah! *(She finds the book.)* Yes, here it is, it arrived from Mudies the other day. *(She brings it down to him.)*

DR. GRIBBLE. *(looking through it)* There's no photograph of Bellingham in this one.

CECILY. Isn't there?

DR. GRIBBLE. Perhaps they're different editions.

CECILY. *(glancing at the photograph in* DR. GRIBBLE*'s book which she is holding)* Who's that like?

DR. GRIBBLE. There's a faint look of Judson, the butcher.

*(*CECILY *listens.)*

CECILY. *(putting* DR. GRIBBLE*'s book on the sofa table and crossing left)* Here's Bruce now. I do hope he won't be –

DR. GRIBBLE. *(rising)* That's all right; I'll ride him on the snaffle, Mrs. Lovell. *(He has left* BRUCE*'s book on the sofa.)*

*(*BRUCE *enters down the stairs, unaware of* DR. GRIBBLE*.)*

BRUCE. Ah, well, thank heavens she's gone! I can't stick people butting in – *(He sees* DR. GRIBBLE*.)*

DR. GRIBBLE. Good evening, Lovell. I just looked in for a little chat, and I've brought you a –

(**BRUCE** *is in a much more erratic state than he was before. He interrupts the* **DOCTOR**.)

BRUCE. *(at the foot of the stairs – with quiet intensity)* What I just said goes for you, too, Dr. Gribble.

DR. GRIBBLE. *(taken aback)* I beg your pardon?

BRUCE. I won't have people butting in.

CECILY. *(left of the table left centre)* Bruce, dear!

DR. GRIBBLE. My dear Lovell, I assure you...

BRUCE. I thought I made it pretty clear yesterday, that it was to be your last visit.

CECILY. But, Bruce, this isn't a visit. Dr. Gribble has very kindly brought –

BRUCE. *(coming down to* **DR. GRIBBLE** *centre)* Oh, don't you tell me – I know you've been conspiring to persuade me not to go away tomorrow. *(a pause)...* Let me tell you, Dr. Gribble, we're going first thing tomorrow sure as I'm standing here. What I've planned, I've planned, and I'm sticking to it; I always do, and I always shall.

CECILY. Bruce, dear, Dr. Gribble has been most considerate, won't you –

BRUCE. *(moving down stage and round left, his back to* **DR. GRIBBLE***)* I'm sick of this place – that's what's wrong with me – this damn constriction – once I'm on a boat again I'll be as right as rain.

(There is a pause, then **DR. GRIBBLE** *makes a fresh effort.)*

DR. GRIBBLE. *(moving to right of the table left centre)* Look here, Lovell – have you thought about your wife? Supposing you're –

BRUCE. Have I got to tell you point-blank to get out? Or – say, is it your account you're worrying about?

CECILY. Bruce!

*(***BRUCE** *and* **DR. GRIBBLE** *are facing each other across the table.)*

BRUCE. If it is, here you are. *(He throws some notes on the table.)* Five pounds for five visits, and that's a good deal more than you usually get around here, and a damn sight more than you're worth.

(There is an extremely awkward silence. Then DR. GRIBBLE draws himself up, turns and moves to the sofa, where he collects his hat, stick and BRUCE's copy of the "Notable Trials" series.)

(CECILY, terribly embarrassed, hurries after the DOCTOR and stops him as he reaches the front door.)

CECILY. *(quietly)* I'm so sorry, doctor.

DR. GRIBBLE. Never mind, Mrs. Lovell – good luck on your travels – good-bye.

CECILY. Thank you, doctor, goodbye

(DR. GRIBBLE goes, closing the front door behind him. There is a pause. CECILY is on the verge of tears.)

Bruce, how could you! To be so rude, and he's such a nice person... *(moving down)* I can't bear to see you get worked up like that... it spoils things so and it's so bad for you.

(She turns, standing centre, and looks out through the French windows. BRUCE comes to her and puts his arm round her tenderly.)

BRUCE. Sorry, dearest, I'm a bit on edge, have been all day. I came down hoping to find us on our own, and it made me just wild when I saw that we weren't... Forgive me, honey... I'll write to the old boy and apologize.

CECILY. Oh, will you?

BRUCE. Sure, I will, tonight, or from the boat tomorrow – oh, it's mean of me to make you unhappy, even for a moment... but you wait and see, I'll be a different person after today – we'll have the grandest time. You've forgiven me?

CECILY. How can I help it?

(He kisses her, then sees his notebook on the sofa table and picks it up.)

BRUCE. Hullo, there's my notebook.

CECILY. Yes, you left it lying about.

(CECILY starts clearing the table left centre and laying it for supper. The cloth, knives and forks, etc., are in the drawer of the table.)

What does nine P.M. mean?

BRUCE. Nine P.M.?

CECILY. It's down in your book for today.

BRUCE. Oh, yes, of course – yes, I'm clearing up the dark room this evening.

CECILY. Ah, I thought it was that.

BRUCE. And you'll help me, my sweetest, won't you?

CECILY. Do you really need me?

BRUCE. Well, why not?

CECILY. I'm sure it's very dirty and dusty down there.

BRUCE. You know me better than that; it's spotless.

CECILY. All right.

BRUCE. *(picking up the rose from the sofa table)* What a lovely rose!

CECILY. *(spreading the tablecloth)* Yes, Hodgson gave it to me when he came to say goodbye. Oh, d'you know, he said that Dunning only asked nine hundred and fifty pounds for this place?

BRUCE. Hodgson said that, did he?

CECILY. *(bringing cruet from the cupboard to the table)* I tried to put him right on the subject, but I don't think I quite convinced him. Darling, you don't think we've been done, do you?

BRUCE. *(wandering across down left to the mirror, tossing the rose on the supper-table as he does so)* Of course not – he's a damned old fool – you know what village gossip is. *(He is looking in the mirror.)*

(CECILY *picks up the rose, kisses it lightly and puts it with the money at* BRUCE*'s place at upstage end of the table.*)

CECILY. *(affectionately)* Bruce, dear, I've been wondering...

BRUCE. *(good-humouredly)* And what have you been wondering?

CECILY. Do you, by any chance, ever use peroxide on your hair?

(He swings round fiercely.)

BRUCE. *(in a sharp uncontrolled voice)* What's that?

CECILY. *(alarmed)* Darling, you *are* jumpy! *(getting knives and forks from the table drawer)* It doesn't matter – it was only a silly personal question.

BRUCE. *(menacingly)* What was that you said?

CECILY. I – I – I only asked if you ever used peroxide on your hair?

BRUCE. *(furiously)* Who's been telling you I dye my hair?

CECILY. It isn't a question of dyeing, I only thought –

BRUCE. *(stepping forward and facing* CECILY *across the table)* It's a lie. Why should I alter the colour of my hair? I'm fair, I've always been fair.

CECILY. Yes, of course, dear.

BRUCE. Well, then?

CECILY. I only thought you might have found a few grey hairs, and wanted to cover them up.

BRUCE. *(very relieved, and trying to laugh it off)* Oh, grey hairs. Oh, I see... I thought you were suggesting that I...

CECILY. What?

BRUCE. *(moving up and round back of the table to centre)* Oh, never mind... don't give it another thought. I've never had a bottle of peroxide in the house.

CECILY. Oh, but how about H_2O_2?

BRUCE. *(sharply)* Well, what about it?

CECILY. Mavis says that's the formula for peroxide.

BRUCE. Damn that girl! What does she want to interfere for?

CECILY. She wasn't interfering – I simply told her that you used it in your developer. You told me, don't you remember?

BRUCE. Oh, yes, of course – yes, I've used it for *that* – you drove it out of my mind with your Billy ideas about hair dye.

CECILY. *(not quite convinced)* Oh, I see. *(soothingly)* In any case, it's of no importance – let's change the subject.

BRUCE. By all means, my dear.

CECILY. How about a drink? *(She goes to the cupboard.)*

BRUCE. Certainly.

CECILY. Oh, we've finished the whisky, I've given the last drop to Hodgson – anyhow, you don't like it much, you'd rather have brandy, wouldn't you? *(She pours it out for him.)*

(BRUCE goes to the top of the table, picks up the money and puts it in his pocket. He then picks up the rose, smells it and puts it in his buttonhole, afterwards sitting in the chair at the head of the table. CECILY gives him his drink.)

BRUCE. O.K. Silly of me to be so rude to old Gribble. Say – I hope he wasn't really scaring you about me going away tomorrow?

(CECILY crosses and gets GRIBBLE's copy of the "Notable Trials" series from the sofa table.)

CECILY. No, no, darling, of course not. As a matter of fact he was rather interesting, and rather funny about the butcher. *(She is standing right of BRUCE's chair, and shows the book open at the photograph.)* Oh, I say, Bruce, who does that remind you of, darling?

(BRUCE stares at it, then puts his glass down heavily on the table with an expression of terror on his face. CECILY starts away from him, terrified.)

CECILY. *(cont.)* Bruce – Bruce, darling, what on earth – ?

BRUCE. *(rising and very ominously advancing towards her as she retreats)* How… How did that photograph get back into my book?

CECILY. Get *back* into – !

BRUCE. I tore it out.

CECILY. Tore it out? But I don't understand.

(He is still advancing very slowly as she retreats.)

BRUCE. I burnt it at the bottom of the garden, the ashes blew away, I saw them – how can they have got back?

CECILY. Bruce, don't look like that. I'll explain. You see, Dr. Gribble is –

(They are both standing facing each other downstage centre CECILY*'s back is semi-turned to the audience.* BRUCE *is upstage and slightly left of her.)*

BRUCE. Ah, so he's in it too, a conspiracy. Gribble, Mavis and you. What are you trying to find out?…

*(*CECILY*'s terrified gaze drops from him for a moment to the photograph, then she raises her eyes again. Ghastly realization steals across her face.)*

Give me the book.

(He snatches it from her. Her hands drop to her sides, but she still stares.)

What's the matter, why are you staring like that?

CECILY. You… you… startled me.

BRUCE. What do you mean – I startled you?

(She realizes that her only chance is to disguise her terror. She begins to act. With a great effort she moves away to the sofa right and, disguising the hysteria in her voice, automatically straightens the sofa cover.)

CECILY. Well, my darling… it's perfectly natural, isn't it! I show you a photograph in the copy of the book Dr. Gribble brought to lend you, not knowing you had it already.

BRUCE. You mean that was old Gribble's book?

CECILY. Of course it was.

BRUCE. *(with great relief)* Well, why in hell didn't you say so before?

CECILY. My dear, you didn't give me a chance, you flared up at me so. I thought you were going to be ill – that was why I was so frightened.

BRUCE. *(convinced)* Oh, I see... yes, it was silly of me, I'm sorry.

CECILY. No, darling, it was silly of me to be such a baby; but you are a little... well, erratic, this evening, aren't you? *(She draws the small window curtains.)*

BRUCE. It's just a mood, you know, you mustn't let me –

CECILY. Oh, I quite understand, it's been a fussy sort of day for you.

BRUCE. Never mind, I shall be all right tomorrow.

(CECILY crosses to the staircase. She is going to try to get upstairs, but BRUCE turns and she stops.)

CECILY. I was silly to look at that sort of book at all – they always frighten me.

BRUCE. You poor kid, it's a shame. That was why I destroyed the photograph in my copy. We'll get rid of this now, shall we? *(He tears the photograph out, throws the book on the sofa and moves to the French windows.)* We'll make sure of it this time.

(He exits into the garden. CECILY stands rooted to the ground for a few moments, then rushes across to the book on the sofa and begins to read it at random, over the upstage arm of the sofa. She reads it with horrified concentration. Then she drops the book in utter repulsion. She crosses to the kitchen door and calls – panic is overcoming her.)

CECILY. *(in a choking voice)* Ethel! Ethel!

(She rushes into the kitchen, then re-enters, snatches her coat from the banisters and runs wildly across to the front door and opens it. **BRUCE** *is standing there.)*

BRUCE. *(quietly)* Hullo, my dear. Where are you off to?

CECILY. I – I've just got to go down to the village for something.

BRUCE. Oh, what?

CECILY. Just a little oil for the salad.

BRUCE. Oh, but the shops will be shut.

CECILY. I could call at the side door of the grocer's.

BRUCE. They'll all be at the fair – besides – it's nearly eight o'clock – it isn't worth it for a drop of oil.

CECILY. I could hurry.

BRUCE. No, my precious, I'd rather you didn't go, there are a lot of undesirable people about; you know what it is with fairs, gypsies and so on. *(He locks the door and puts the key in his pocket.)* Heaven knows who may be prowling about. *(He takes* **CECILY**'s *coat from her, puts it on the sofa, then closes the French windows and draws the curtains.)* We'd better be on the safe side.

CECILY. Yes, you're quite right. I'd no idea it was so late. I'd better get the supper. *(She moves to the kitchen.)*

BRUCE. I'll come and help you. *(He joins her.)*

(She stops a moment, swaying.)

What's the matter?

*(**CECILY** is clutching the chair left of the table, her back towards **BRUCE** who stands in front of the kitchen door watching her.)*

CECILY. *(recovering herself)* Nothing... nothing, I just felt a little faint for a moment, that's all.

BRUCE. Ah, you want some food, that's what it is... it'll never do to have you feeling faint, will it, sweetheart?

CECILY. *(turning and facing him)* No, no, of course not. *(She braces herself.)* I'm all right now – I look all right, don't I?

BRUCE. Yes, rather, you look swell.

CECILY. Good… come on, let's get supper.

(BRUCE *comes forward, puts his right arm round her shoulders, and they move off to the kitchen as the lights fade to blackness, after which –*)

(*The curtain falls*)

Scene II

(Scene – The same. About half an hour later.)

(BRUCE and CECILY are seated at the supper-table; BRUCE up stage, CECILY on his left. They have just finished.)

(The curtains are still drawn.)

(BRUCE, who is now quite insane, is in a condition of happy self-aggrandizement.)

BRUCE. A remarkably good supper... extraordinarily clever of you to have taught Ethel to make chicken-salad so well.

CECILY. I'm glad you enjoyed it

BRUCE. So am I; after all, tonight is a special occasion – a celebration.

CECILY. Of course – yes- – we're going away tomorrow.

(BRUCE laughs.)

What are you laughing at?

BRUCE. Nothing, nothing.

CECILY. Have some more brandy. *(She passes the brandy bottle, which is on the table.)*

BRUCE. No, thank you – I believe you're trying to make me drunk – you couldn't do that. I've got a very strong head.

CECILY. Oh, but you've only had two brandies.

BRUCE. That's quite enough. There's a funny sort of buzzing in my head – more than buzzing, pounding – it's all right, I've had it before – just the excitement – *(she looks at him)* – of going away tomorrow.

CECILY. Don't you think you'd better finish your packing?

BRUCE. *(rising)* That reminds me – I found the key of the clock in the pocket of one of my suits... *(He moves upstage.)* I'll wind the old clock now. What's the time?

CECILY. *(looking at her watch)* A quarter to nine. But it's hardly worth it if we're going away tomorrow.

BRUCE. *(at the clock, his back to the audience)* It gives me a strange sort of thrill always to see the minutes slipping by on the face of a grandfather clock. *(He continues as he winds it.)* I can remember so well, standing in my headmaster's study at school, waiting for a beating, and seeing the hands move on – nothing I could do could stop them.

(CECILY *rises and steals off to the kitchen.* BRUCE *does not apparently notice her.)*

I can remember the funny mixture of sensations it used to give me... terror, and yet with it a strange sort of delight. I locked that back door, dear, when we were getting the supper.

(He turns, then absently wanders back to his place at the table. There is a pause. CECILY *enters with coffee and two cups on a tray.)*

CECILY. I was just fetching the coffee.

(She puts the tray down on the table, watching him furtively. His hands are at his head again. She pours out a cup and hands it to him.)

Here's your coffee.

BRUCE. *(absently)* What?

CECILY. Here's your coffee.

BRUCE. Oh – yes – how far away your voice sounds – it must be my head.

CECILY. Don't you think you'd better lie down?

BRUCE. Oh, no, it's not *unpleasant!* I'm afraid you've been wasting your sympathy over my little attacks, my dear. It may sound funny to you, but d'you know they're almost enjoyable... The sense of pace inside one, the pounding faster and faster, becomes almost music – wild, rushing music... The outlines of things become blurred, but their colours sharper... What's the time now?

CECILY. Ten minutes to nine.

BRUCE. No, it's more surely – eight minutes to, nearly seven, isn't it?

CECILY. No, dear, only just ten to.

BRUCE. We must be getting to work soon.

CECILY. Don't you think it would be better not to do any more this evening...

BRUCE. No, I've made my plans. I never alter my plans.

CECILY. *(calmly)* Oh, all right.

BRUCE. You're a sensible girl, aren't you?

CECILY. How do you mean?

BRUCE. You don't "go on" at a man. Very few women can say "Oh, all right," and leave it at that... But, then, most women are fools. *(He smiles to himself.)*

CECILY. *(trying to be conversational)* Do you think so?

BRUCE. I don't think, I know – born fools!...

CECILY. Perhaps you're right.

BRUCE. And woman's weakness is man's opportunity. Did someone write that, or did I think of it myself? – If I did it's good – damn good! – "Woman's weakness is man's opportunity."

CECILY. You have extraordinary insight into things... Have some more coffee.

BRUCE. Please... Yes, you're right, I have great insight. I've a lot of power over women. I discovered quite early in life that I could twist women round my little finger. It's a useful gift.

CECILY. It must be.

BRUCE. Boyish – that's the note they like – makes them feel sort of maternal... It gets them every time – and if you can be slightly different from their own men folk...

CECILY. How?

BRUCE. Well, in America, for instance, English – with a slight drawl and possibly a title thrown in. And in England – a colonial, or vaguely American type, goes down well, a suggestion of adventurous "He-man"... the prairies and so on... that seems to do the trick. I thought it would as soon as the house-agent told me about you letting your flat, because you'd won the Sweep, and then when I saw you – Real romance, wasn't it? *(He takes her hands.)* Happy ever after.

CECILY. *(rising)* It's rather airless in here. Oh, we've got all the doors and windows shut – I feel quite breathless.

(BRUCE rises and very gently puts CECILY back in her cliair.)

BRUCE. Why, you're shivering. You don't want that night air – what you need is a cup of coffee. It'll do you good.

(He pours her out some, then, humming the "Merry Widow" waltz, wanders over into the shadows on the right of the stage and picks up DR. GRIBBLE's book from the sofa. His voice comes loudly and quickly out of the darkness.)

A strange coincidence, Dr. Gribble reading the same book as me... I wonder if, by any chance... Oh, no, of course not – still it was a funny coincidence.

CECILY. Yes, wasn't it?

BRUCE. I wonder what he makes of it all. They're nearly always so hopelessly wrong. They say most murderers are mad – that they've got a kink somewhere – that's nonsense. A murderer is often a man who's a bit saner than other people – Don't you agree?

CECILY. Yes, I dare say... certainly.

BRUCE. *(still with the book)* Armstrong was clever, but not clever enough; Palmer of Rugeley became over-confident – they all get like that and it's fatal... Now, Bellingham here, what do you think of Bellingham, my dear?

CECILY. You know I don't study these things – I know nothing about him.

BRUCE. No? A pity – he's well worth studying – he's the cleverest of the lot. He never makes a mistake. Women have fallen for him every time, they've gone to the country with him, they've signed away their fortunes. *(He comes back to the table with the book.)*

CECILY. He must be very clever.

BRUCE. He's a genius. Did old Gribble discuss the case with you?

CECILY. *(absently)* I don't know – oh, yes – yes – he said something about the case being unique.

(BRUCE lights a cigarette from the box on the table, then sits in his chair again.)

BRUCE. Did he? Well, he's quite right, it certainly was – it certainly is... What I can't get over is us both reading the book at the same time.

CECILY. Oh, I don't know. You're both interested in – the same subject – you both read the new books on it.

BRUCE. But today, of all days.

CECILY. Why?

BRUCE. *(putting down the book)* Oh, never mind.

CECILY. *(rising and making for the stairs)* Really, Bruce, if you don't mind I think I'll go to bed now – I'm terribly tired.

BRUCE. *(catching her left arm and stopping her)* No, you're forgetting, you promised to help me. Sit down. I've got an idea. Read to me – out of this book. *(He puts the book in front of her.)* Thousands and thousands must have read it, may be reading it now and one can't see or hear them – such a pity! Yes – yes, that's a good idea – read to me about Bellingham. Begin at the introduction – it's got all the best part of it there.

(BRUCE turns his chair slightly instage, puts in an eyeglass which he has taken from his pocket, and settles back with an air of comfortable self-aggrandizement to enjoy the reading.)

CECILY. *(reading quickly and automatically from the book, which is open on the table in front of her)* "George Edward

Bellingham, to give him the name by which he was tried, for his real name is still unknown –

(**BRUCE** *chuckles.*)

– has a multitude of aliases, and has been popularly nicknamed 'Frankie' Bellingham, 'The Californian Bluebeard.' He was acquitted on an attempted murder charge owing to insufficient evidence and the brilliance of his defence, although he was suspected of having done away with no less than five young women."

BRUCE. (*speaking through her reading*) Five – pooh!

CECILY. "After his acquittal Bellingham disappeared, and three months later overwhelming evidence against him came to light."

BRUCE. Louder, please!

CECILY. "The bodies of four of his victims were discovered buried under the cellars of various houses he had rented from time to time."

BRUCE. Can't you speak louder?

CECILY. (*very loudly*) "He would make the acquaintance of a girl, persuade her to marry after a few weeks, or even days. He would induce her to sign papers making over to him any sum of money she might have."

BRUCE. I still can't hear you.

CECILY. (*almost shouting*) "It was his habit to rent a small place in an out-of-the-way neighbourhood. After living there for two or three months, he would announce to neighbours or acquaintances that he and his wife were going abroad for some time. The fact that the Mrs. Bellingham of the moment was never actually seen to leave the place seems to have awakened no suspicion. Yet in every case the cellar could have told a guilty secret, and if – " (*She falters in her reading.*) Tell me, Bruce – do you think that supposing one of these women had found out beforehand and had made an appeal to him, she could have stopped him?

BRUCE. Why do you ask?

(Mechanically she picks up the cigarette-box and takes out a cigarette. She leaves the box on her lap and during the ensuing scene she fidgets with the cigarette and tears it to pieces.)

CECILY. Well, it's interesting to know how that sort of man's mind works. Do you think if he'd been fond of the woman – and I suppose he was fond of some of them –

BRUCE. Oh, yes, a bit, certainly.

CECILY. Well, then, don't you think he might have listened to an appeal?

BRUCE. The situation never arose – I should imagine. But no – no, I'm quite sure he wouldn't have let anything influence him.

CECILY. But if, as you say, he'd cared –

BRUCE. But – you don't understand – it was his profession – these women represented to him certain sums of money.

CECILY. I see. But supposing if she'd said to him – "Look here, I know who you are and what you're after, I am at your mercy, you can take my money – all of it – "

BRUCE. Ah, but he'd got their money already.

CECILY. Yes, but if she'd said, "I don't mind. You're robbing me of every penny I possess. If only you'll let me go, I won't attempt to prosecute you, I won't inform the police" – what do you suppose he would have said?

BRUCE. He'd never have let her go. *(with a laugh)* Can you imagine any man risking his life on a woman's silence?

CECILY. And yet, you'd think he'd be glad of any chance of escaping the horror of the actual... but then... perhaps it didn't seem – perhaps there wasn't any horror in it for him?

BRUCE. *(dreamily)* No. You see there are other sides to it. Power – the climax of the music – a feeling that is almost God-like – one moment to hold someone in your arms and the next moment to hold *something*.

(The clock begins to strike nine.)

(**BRUCE** *rises very slowly and moves equally slowly round to the clock. His attention is riveted on it – he is fascinated.* **CECILY**, *her gaze wandering round in a caged, desperate fashion, becomes aware of the cigarette-box in her lap. She picks it up and from it suddenly gets an idea. She has just time to convey a wild hope when* **BRUCE** *begins to come towards her.*)

BRUCE. *(speaking violently)* Now!

CECILY. No! Wait! I've got something to tell you.

BRUCE. I don't want to hear.

CECILY. This is important – it's about murder!

BRUCE. *(checked)* Eh?

CECILY. I know it'll interest you – it must – because it concerns you – vitally.

BRUCE. What?

CECILY. Listen, Bruce, it would be a queer thing, wouldn't it, if a murderer were to marry a murderess?

BRUCE. That's a strange idea.

CECILY. Yes, indeed – far stranger than anything in *The Arabian Nights* – yet it's true.

(Her intensity compels him.)

(rising and standing at the back of her chair – thinking desperately) It's my own story, Bruce. I've killed a man, and I've never been found out.

BRUCE. Have you? *(He is interested in spite of himself, and sits.)*

CECILY. You know what it's like, you must know what it's like, to hide a secret like that.

BRUCE. Yes, it's almost unbearable sometimes –

CECILY. Well – well… To begin with, I've been married before. No one knew about it except my mother.

BRUCE. When was this?

CECILY. When I was eighteen. I was his secretary. He had money. I was terribly tired of being poor and I thought it was a way out. But he was mean – horribly mean. He used to grudge me every penny. It was he who put the idea into my head. He used to say, "If we're careful now, there'll be all the more for me to leave you when I die."

BRUCE. Where did all this happen?

CECILY. Er – on the East Coast – a horrible little place – the wind never seemed to stop blowing.

BRUCE. Go on.

CECILY. I turned plan after plan over in my mind and at last my opportunity came.

BRUCE. Poison? Women usually use poison.

CECILY. No, it was something much safer than that. That winter he was taken seriously ill. The doctor said it was pneumonia. I pretended to be heart-broken – it deceived everybody. Even in his illness, my husband's meanness got the better of him. He would only have one nurse, so I relieved her at night. Everyone remarked on my devotion – I took care of that.

BRUCE. That was clever of you.

CECILY. The doctor gave me the most careful instructions – the warmth of the room and so on. One night, when I was alone with him, the crisis came. I knelt down by his bedside and prayed that he would die. I must have been on my knees a long time – when I looked up I saw that he had sunk into a deep sleep. The crisis was over and he was going to get better. I went to the window. I can see myself now, standing there – the frost had made such pretty patterns on the window-panes – standing there, making up my mind.

(There is a pause.)

BRUCE. You opened the window?

CECILY. The air was like a knife. I stripped the bed-clothes off him and left the door open. It didn't take very long. When I went back into the room he was dead. I closed the window, made up the fire – I even put fresh hot-water-bottles in the bed. Then I 'phoned the doctor.

(There is another pause.)

BRUCE. No one suspected?

CECILY. Not a thing. The doctor – everyone – was terribly sorry for me.

BRUCE. And the money?

CECILY. Er – I was rather foolish about that – it didn't last very long.

BRUCE. I understand that so well. *(He rises.)* But there's just one thing I don't understand. Why have you been telling me all this now?

CECILY. Well, don't you see – you know all about me now – I can't possibly give you away – I thought perhaps we might be useful to each other.

BRUCE. Yes – yes, that would be rather a good idea – if only there was a grain of truth in your story! *(He pauses.)* Very clever of you, Cecily, arousing my interest and trying to put me off. *(He turns away centre, helpless with laughter as he speaks.)* I know where you got the story from – I've read the book myself…

(CECILY backs away to the oak beam by the cellar. BRUCE is roaring, doubled up with laughter. He moves back towards the table.)

… and I remember that bit about the hot-water-bottles, struck me as such a clever idea. *(He laughs.)* You, *you* – opening the windows and waiting for him to die! You didn't really expect me to believe that story, did you?

CECILY. *(moving to the table and speaking with desperate calmness)* No! I never for one moment expected you to believe it. I didn't care whether you did or not.

BRUCE. *What?* Didn't care – ?

CECILY. There's something you've forgotten… I didn't drink any coffee!

BRUCE. Coffee? What has that got to do with it?

CECILY. I only wanted to hold your attention for a little while – to gain time –

BRUCE. Time for what?

CECILY. Time for the stuff to work.

BRUCE. *(standing frozen with growing horror)* I don't believe it – it's another story – you couldn't – !

CECILY. You were right – it was a funny coincidence Dr. Gribble reading that book.

BRUCE. Gribble? He – you mean he gave you…? *(Convinced, he collapses into his chair.)*

CECILY. *(pouncing on him and grabbing him by the lapels of his coat)* Yes, that's it. It's so simple, don't you see. He's been attending you for some time – there'll be no need for any inquiry.

BRUCE. Inquiry? You… You… !

CECILY. Now it's taking effect – it's beginning to choke you! It's starting to paralyse you – you can't move, can you? You can't move.

BRUCE. *(choking)* I… *(He shakes his head.)* I…

CECILY. You're going numb and cold now – it's stealing all over you… You can't move hand or foot –

(There is a terrible rasping noise in BRUCE's throat. CECILY, her eyes fixed on him in horror, backs away from him to the post by the cellar. As she gets there there is a loud knocking on the front door. She rushes to the door. NIGEL's voice is heard outside.)

NIGEL. *(off)* Cecily, Cecily, are you there?

CECILY. *(screaming hysterically)* Nigel! Nigel! Help me! Quickly! *(She struggles with the handle.)* God! It's locked! He's got the key! I can't – ! Let me out! Let me out! I can't bear it! I shall go mad! *(She is hammering loudly on the door and screaming.)*

(There is a smash of glass. NIGEL opens the French window and enters. He takes in the scene at a glance and rushes straight to CECILY. MAVIS follows him.)

NIGEL. It's all right, darling – Quiet! Quiet! You're quite safe now.

MAVIS. Thank God we came back!

CECILY. *(screaming hysterically)* Take me out! Take me out!

(**NIGEL** *puts his arm round her and leads her to the window.*)

NIGEL. It's all right, darling – it's all right – we're with you – he can't touch you now – it's all right.

(**CECILY***'s screams fade in the distance. There is silence.* **BRUCE***'s body relaxes and slumps in the chair as – *)

(curtain)

FURNITURE AND PROPERTY PLOT

ACT ONE

Scene I

The following properties are essential:

Bureau.

>*In it:*
>> Sealed note to Nigel in downstage top small drawer.
>> Inventory in pigeonhole.
>> Notebook and pencil on flap.

Mantelpiece.

>*On it:*
>> 2 candlesticks.
>> Box of matches.
>> Ashtray.
>> Shilling on downstage end.

Table centre.

>*On it:*
>> Old sheets of newspaper.
>> Duster.
>> Book cigarette-box with cigarettes.
>> Ashtray with match-stand.
>> Sheets of new tissue-paper.

AUNTIE LOO-LOO's coat, bag and gloves on bureau chair.

Small trunk centre stage.

Telephone on table l.

Ashtray and matches on small table in front of sofa

MAVIS's bag and gloves on window-seat

Offstage left centre:

> MAVIS's hat and coat.
> Small dressing-table drawer lined with newspaper.
> Sheets.
> Miscellaneous linen.

Offstage right centre:

> One-pound note for CECILY's handbag.
> 3 small parcels for CECILY.
> Notebook and pencil for BRUCE.

Scene II

Strike CECILY's parcels from table centre

Strike CECILY's coat and hat from armchair left.

Move small drawer from table to floor downstage of bureau.

Re-set bureau chair.

Provide NIGEL with open envelope with written note inside.

Offstage left centre:

Walking-shoes for CECILY.

Offstage right centre:

Carrier-bag from Harrods for AUNTIE LOO-LOO.

ACT TWO

Scene I

For this scene the stage should not look so tidy and the setting given below should be followed.

The upholstered armchair should be set up stage right of the table left centre and facing down centre.

The small table in front of the sofa to be set at the left arm of the sofa.

The armchair down right to be set just right of the fireplace, to correspond to the chair set left of the fireplace.

French windows closed and curtains closed.

2 rugs folded on fender.

Small pair of steps by window up right.

Standing mirror lying on cupboard up left centre

Handbell on window-ledge of window up right.

Lower flap of gate-legged table down.

On gate-legged table:

Sharp knife for cutting string, blotting-paper, corrugated paper, bills, circulars, etc.

Tin box on floor below gate-legged table, packed with Chinese shawl and photograph album; also miscellaneous packing.

Trunk from Act I on floor up stage centre, packed with 2 cushions, the wrapped candlesticks and 1 dozen books.

Offstage left:

Parcel containing 6 books for ETHEL.

Vase for ETHEL.

Offstage right

> Frontdoor key for CECILY.
>
> Small parcels for CECILY.
>
> 2 legal documents and fountain-pen for BRUCE.
>
> Gardening book for AUNTIE LOO-LOO.
>
> Bunch of white and mauve lilac for HODGSON.

Scene II

The following are the essential properties:

Book cigarette-box, ashtray and box of matches on table left centre

Tea-tray on small table in front of sofa.

> *On tray:*
>
> 2 cups, 2 saucers, 2 spoons, milk-jug with milk, sugar-basin with sugar, plate of bread and butter, plate of sponge-cakes, glass jar containing cigarettes, matches,

Newspaper on top of cupboard up left centre

Mirror on wall down left.

Offstage left:

> Teapot containing tea, and hot-water jug for ETHEL.
>
> Photographic dish with snaps for BRUCE.
>
> Notebook for BRUCE.
>
> 4 letters and salver for ETHEL.

Offstage right:

> Gardening gloves and silk scarf for CECILY.
>
> Small earth-stained sack containing peroxide bottles and rag for HODGSON.
>
> Case for DR. GRIBBLE.

ACT THREE

Scene I

Move small armchair from down right to right of fireplace.

Set upholstered armchair down right.

Set small table in front of sofa to left of sofa.

Bring chair from left of fireplace to above table left.

Strike all flowers.

Re-set book cigarette-box and matches on table left centre

Check knives, forks and table-cloth in drawer of table.

Set tray with 3 glasses, bottle of whisky (nearly empty) and syphon on bop of cupboard.

Check bottle of brandy, tumbler and cruet stand in cupboard.

Place BRUCE's notebook on sofa.

Set second Bellingham book (without photo) in bookcase.

Offstage left:

    Wad of one-pound notes for BRUCE.

    Key of grandfather clock for BRUCE.

    Eyeglass for BRUCE.

Offstage right

    Dog's-lead for CECILY.

    Cigarette-case and matches in handbag for MAVIS.

    Bunch of herbaceous flowers for HODGSON.

    Single rose for HODGSON.

    Copy of Bellingham book with photograph for DR. CRIBBLE.

Scene II

Strike tray of drinks from cupboard.

Remains of salad in bowl (with servers), 2 dirty plates, knives and forks on cupboard.

2 glasses, crumbled bread, etc, on tablo left centre

Offstage left:

    Pot of black coffee, sugar, 2 cups, saucers and spoons, on tray for CECILY.

CPSIA information can be obtained
at www.ICGtesting.com
Printed in the USA
LVOW01s2314190916
505330LV00031B/654/P